MW01602001

BRUNHILD

AND KRIEMHILD

Yuiko Agarizaki

Illustration by **Aoaso**

Brunhild and her sister Kriemhild's strange
and cruel fate—they served the kingdom and were
erased from its history.

BRUNHILD

AND KRIEMHILD

CONTENTS

Illustration: Aoaso

Original Cover Design: Shunya Fujita (Tsuyoshi Kusano Design)

Yen Press Cover Design: Eddy Mingki

Bernstein

A human who was turned into an amber dragon by an evil dragon's sorcery, he was sealed in a basement beneath the kingdom during the reign of the First Queen.

...Please fly my sister away on your wings. There is no place for her here in this kingdom.

Warren

The Queen's chief vassal, having served her since the generation of the First, the one called the Dragonslaying Queen. This old soldier is the only man in the nation capable of killing a dragon.

Kriemhild

Daughter of the Fifth Queen, and Brunhild's younger sister. She took the throne in place of her sister when she fell ill and, on the day of her crowning ceremony, learns of the kingdom's dark secrets.

BRUNHILD AND KRIEMHILD

Brunhild

Daughter of the Fifth Queen, and Kriemhild's older sister. A year before she would have succeeded the throne, she fell ill, unable to bear the burden of God's power. And while it pains her, she has left succession to her younger sister.

So long as we do not defeat Warren, we have no future. We'll think of a new way for the kingdom to be.

If you flinch just to see me, then defeating Warren is but a faraway dream.

I'll do everything I can. 'Cause that's all I can do.

Anima

A young junior soldier of the kingdom who dreams of an ordinary life. Born from the lineage of the evil dragon Sigurd, who was vanquished by the First Queen, he goes by a fake name to avoid persecution.

AND KRIEMHILD

BRUNHILD

Yuiko Agarizaki

Illustration by **Aoaso**

nhild and her sister
emhild's strange and cruel
e—they served the kingdom
were erased from its
tory.

YEN
ON

New York

BRUNHILD
AND KRIEMHILD

Yuiko Agarizaki

Translation by Jennifer Ward † Cover art by Aoaso

This book is a work of fiction. Names, characters, places, and incidents are
the product of the author's imagination or are used fictitiously. Any resemblance to
actual events, locales, or persons, living or dead, is coincidental.

KRIEMHILD TO BRUNHILD
©Yuiko Agarizaki 2023
Edited by Dengeki Bunko
First published in Japan in 2023 by KADOKAWA CORPORATION, Tokyo.
English translation rights arranged with KADOKAWA CORPORATION, Tokyo, through Tuttle-Mori
Agency, Inc., Tokyo.

English translation © 2025 by Yen Press, LLC

Yen Press, LLC supports the right to free expression and the value of copyright. The purpose of copyright is to
encourage writers and artists to produce the creative works that enrich our culture.

The scanning, uploading, and distribution of this book without permission is a theft of the author's intellectual
property. If you would like permission to use material from the book (other than for review purposes), please
contact the publisher. Thank you for your support of the author's rights.

Yen On
150 West 30th Street, 6th Floor
New York, NY 10001

Visit us at yenpress.com † facebook.com/yenpress † twitter.com/yenpress †
yenpress.tumblr.com † instagram.com/yenpress

First Yen On Edition: February 2025
Edited by Yen On Editorial: Payton Campbell
Designed by Yen Press Design: Eddy Mingki

Yen On is an imprint of Yen Press, LLC.
The Yen On name and logo are trademarks of Yen Press, LLC.

The publisher is not responsible for websites (or their content) that are not owned by the publisher.

Library of Congress Cataloging-in-Publication Data
Names: Agarizaki, Yuiko, author. | Aoaso, illustrator. | Ward, Jennifer, translator.
Title: Brunhild the dragonslayer / Yuiko Agarizaki ; illustration by Aoaso ; translation by Jennifer Ward.
Other titles: Ryuugoroshi no Brunhild. English
Description: First Yen On edition. | New York, NY : Yen On, 2024–
Identifiers: LCCN 2023057875 | ISBN 9781975378929 (v. 1 ; hardcover) |
ISBN 9781975394844 (v. 2 ; hardcover)
Subjects: CYAC: Fantasy. | LCGFT: Fantasy fiction. | Light novels.
LC record available at https://lccn.loc.gov/2023057875

ISBNs: 979-8-8554-1082-2 (hardcover)
979-8-8554-1083-9 (ebook)

10 9 8 7 6 5 4 3 2 1

LSC-C

Printed in the United States of America

A N D   K R I E M H I L D

BRUNHILD

uiko Agarizaki
ustration by **Aoaso**

nhild and her sister
emhild's strange and cruel
—they served the kingdom
were erased from its
ory.

YEN
ON
New York

BRUNHILD

AND KRIEMHILD

Yuiko Agarizaki

Translation by Jennifer Ward † Cover art by Aoaso

This book is a work of fiction. Names, characters, places, and incidents are
the product of the author's imagination or are used fictitiously. Any resemblance to
actual events, locales, or persons, living or dead, is coincidental.

KRIEMHILD TO BRUNHILD
©Yuiko Agarizaki 2023
Edited by Dengeki Bunko
First published in Japan in 2023 by KADOKAWA CORPORATION, Tokyo.
English translation rights arranged with KADOKAWA CORPORATION, Tokyo, through Tuttle-Mori
Agency, Inc., Tokyo.

English translation © 2025 by Yen Press, LLC

Yen Press, LLC supports the right to free expression and the value of copyright. The purpose of copyright is to
encourage writers and artists to produce the creative works that enrich our culture.

The scanning, uploading, and distribution of this book without permission is a theft of the author's intellectual
property. If you would like permission to use material from the book (other than for review purposes), please
contact the publisher. Thank you for your support of the author's rights.

Yen On
150 West 30th Street, 6th Floor
New York, NY 10001

Visit us at yenpress.com † facebook.com/yenpress † twitter.com/yenpress †
yenpress.tumblr.com † instagram.com/yenpress

First Yen On Edition: February 2025
Edited by Yen On Editorial: Payton Campbell
Designed by Yen Press Design: Eddy Mingki

Yen On is an imprint of Yen Press, LLC.
The Yen On name and logo are trademarks of Yen Press, LLC.

The publisher is not responsible for websites (or their content) that are not owned by the publisher.

Library of Congress Cataloging-in-Publication Data
Names: Agarizaki, Yuiko, author. | Aoaso, illustrator. | Ward, Jennifer, translator.
Title: Brunhild the dragonslayer / Yuiko Agarizaki ; illustration by Aoaso ; translation by Jennifer Ward.
Other titles: Ryuugoroshi no Brunhild. English
Description: First Yen On edition. | New York, NY : Yen On, 2024–
Identifiers: LCCN 2023057875 | ISBN 9781975378929 (v. 1 ; hardcover) |
ISBN 9781975394844 (v. 2 ; hardcover)
Subjects: CYAC: Fantasy. | LCGFT: Fantasy fiction. | Light novels.
LC record available at https://lccn.loc.gov/2023057875

ISBNs: 979-8-8554-1082-2 (hardcover)
979-8-8554-1083-9 (ebook)

10 9 8 7 6 5 4 3 2 1

LSC-C

Printed in the United States of America

Chapter

1

There was once a kingdom ruled by the Dragonslaying Queen—Queen Siegfried.

This dragonslayer was the child of God. Even when she had been mortal, she'd been as close to divinity as one could be.

This girl had once been the Dragon Priestess.

With the "Power of God" contained in her body, she had destroyed the evil dragon that had controlled the kingdom—though at the time, he had been calling himself the Divine Dragon—and became the queen.

The Dragonslaying Queen was kind. She prioritized the happiness of the people, and she accomplished many great feats. Not only did she free the people from the control of the evil dragon, she also destroyed the other dragons lurking within the kingdom, abolished discriminatory customs that had persisted from archaic ways of life, drove away aggressive foreign powers with her Thunder, and also developed the nation by engaging in trade with friendly countries.

Nearly a hundred years had passed since the queen had killed the evil dragon.

The two daughters of the Fifth Queen were in a room littered with dresses.

"Hmm, I wonder which one would best suit my little sister." The thirteen-year-old Brunhild compared the dress she held in her right hand to the one in her left. "Hmm, I'm sure both would suit you. You're *my* little sister, after all."

"Sister… I have to get changed, soon," the other girl said hesitantly. Her name was Kriemhild, and she was Brunhild's younger sister by one year. Her timidity showed in her quiet voice. She had been waiting for about an hour now in her underclothes for her older sister to finish choosing her outfit.

Both girls had black hair and black eyes. That was typical of the Siegfried family daughters.

"If we spend any more time on this, we shall be late for the party," said Kriemhild.

That day, a party in commemoration of the birth of the First Queen would be held among the royal family and nobles.

Brunhild told her not to take her eyes off the clothes in her hands. "It's fine to be a little bit late. We're the daughters of the royal Siegfried family."

"We can't act conceited just because we're royals…"

"This is because our future spouses might be there, you know? Powerful nobles from all over the kingdom will be gathering today. I've heard it was at this very event that Mother found Father. So when we go to today's party, we should be attired in our very finest, even if we're late. You might even fall in love at first sight or have someone fall in love with you, Kriemhild."

"Th-that won't happen." Kriemhild's cheeks were a little pink. "I'm still only twelve…"

"You mean you're *already* twelve… Yes, I've made up my mind on this dress."

Brunhild decided to have her sister wear the dress in her right hand. The younger sister, in her underclothes, was relieved she could finally put something on. Brunhild began to dress her sister. It was a complicated process to put on one of these royal dresses, and being quite the task, the girls typically had maids dress them. But today, Brunhild wouldn't leave her sister's attire to a maid. She loved to dress up her sister herself, and she believed she could attire her more beautifully than anyone else.

"I understand you best, after all…"

Finally, Kriemhild was all dressed up.

The girl in her underclothes had been transformed into a princess in a fashionable dress.

Looking at her sister, Brunhild was satisfied. "Mm-hmm. As beautiful as a portrait, if I may say so of my own sister."

"You're exaggerating."

The elder sister suddenly embraced her timid younger sister.

"Sister, what are you doing…?"

"You're going to be lonely, aren't you? Now that you've grown to be so beautiful… The day when you'll leave me is not far off."

These two sisters had grown up not knowing the love of a father and mother.

Their father died soon after the girls had been born. Their mother had been busy every day with her duties as the queen. She had assigned many maids and servants to them, and they had grown up wanting for nothing, but no matter how many servants they were given, a stranger was still a stranger. They could not replace their family.

Given their situation, naturally Brunhild had come to feel that she had to take care of her sister herself, and the younger sister had come to rely on her even more than their mother.

"You should just become the king, Kriemhild. And then I'll be the queen. Then we'll be together forever."

"You jest." Kriemhild smiled wryly. "But that does sound wonderful. Since at the very least right now, I cannot imagine a future apart from you. No matter what sort of boy might fall for me."

Brunhild gave Kriemhild a spontaneous, squeezing hug. "What an adorable thing of you to say."

They stayed like that a moment, but eventually, Brunhild drew away from her sister and said, "It's time to go. I really would feel bad for them if we kept the carriage waiting any longer."

The two of them headed for the carriage to leave the royal villa. By the time they got in, it was already two hours past the time when they were supposed to have left. The coachman seemed quite irritated at having been made to wait so long, making Kriemhild feel apologetic.

With their knight escort, the carriage proceeded to the venue. It was customary for this party to be held at the private residence of the former royal family.

They approached the road up the hill.

When Kriemhild happened to look out the window to the side, she saw the mounted knights who were riding beside them.

Inside the carriage, Kriemhild asked Brunhild, "Do we need such a strict guard?"

"I'm sure it's just in case… There have been more battles with foreign nations lately."

Their kingdom was not a very big one. However, there were technologies and energy that existed only within this land. These past ten years, there had been a sharp increase in invasions from foreign armies after these resources.

"The influence of the First Queen is declining."

The First Queen had had the greatest power of all the generations of queens, and she had repelled all the attacking foreign armies with incredible martial might that could be called supernatural. Ever since, nations that attacked the kingdom had not lasted long, but the First Queen had passed away over seventy years ago now.

The fear of their kingdom was slowly fading away.

"It is. We must be careful. We two are some of those unique technologies and energy that foreign lands seek, after all."

The Siegfried family had an extremely unique bloodline. Due to various events of the past, the clan had come to have a mysterious energy known as the "Power of God" within them. From this "Power of God," the Siegfried clan were endowed with various unique abilities. For that reason, foreign nations desired people of the Siegfried family as research material.

Brunhild did not miss Kriemhild's uneasy expression. She took her sister's hand and said, "You need not be so afraid. Even if on the rare chance we were to be attacked, I shall protect you."

Kriemhild gave a faint smile. It seemed as if her fear had eased just a little. "Yes, if you'll protect me, then there's nothing for me to fear."

She looked out the window. She could see the knights riding alongside them. "And there are so many knights with us, too…"

Her remark trailed off.

Because there was a splashing sound, and red fluid dirtied the window.

Their knight guards were being attacked.

Kriemhild let out a tiny shriek. "Yeep…!"

A monster that looked like a lion was outside the window. That creature, which had leaped out from the ravine, had just crushed a knight's neck in its teeth.

The lion's eyes moved. It glared at Kriemhild in the carriage. Their gazes locked.

Brunhild yanked Kriemhild toward her and covered her body with her own.

A moment later, the carriage swayed wildly. They could tell that the grotesque lion-creature had body-slammed the carriage.

"Yeeeeeeeeeeeeeeeeek!"

Kriemhild's cry rang out in the carriage. Brunhild held her tight, trying to protect her from the impact.

Their field of view spun. The carriage had toppled over. The sisters were struck with a hard impact, but neither were injured. Having inherited the Power of God, both of them were physically exceptional and wouldn't be wounded by the normal laws of physics.

Even after toppling over, the carriage rattled terribly. Something outside seemed to be shaking it.

Through the walls, they could hear screams and the growls of fierce beasts. The dying cries were most likely those of the coachman and their knight guards.

The lion-creature tore the door of the carriage with its claws, creating the shape of a crescent moon. Light poured in.

Through the gashes, the beast peered in at the two of them.

The large fangs peeking from its mouth were wet with blood. Red droplets were dripping down. Brunhild calmly pulled Kriemhild deeper into the carriage. All Kriemhild could do was cry out in fear.

"Ah…ahh!! Wahh…"

As Kriemhild was panicking, Brunhild tried to somehow guard her behind her back.

The lion-creature began destroying the carriage. The tears it had slashed open widened, and its large grotesque face drew closer to the pair.

"Hyee…no…"

The creature snapped its jaws around Kriemhild and dragged her out of the carriage.

"Sister, Sister!"

"Kriemhild!"

Brunhild followed, leaving the carriage as well.

Outside the carriage, a battle was raging. The surviving knights who had been defending the princesses had drawn their swords, fighting against their attackers along the mountain path. The attackers commanded countless grotesque beasts. This was a sorcery that didn't exist in this kingdom. Based on that, Brunhild surmised the attackers were foreigners.

The situation was not favorable for the knights.

Countless horrific creatures had knocked over the carriage, and they had killed most of the knights who had been defending it. It seemed the knights' sturdy armor had been no use at all in the face of their ferocious fangs.

The only strength the knights had was the secret remedy unique to their kingdom, the "Miracle of Life."

It was a drug that would cure any injury. Knights were using the Miracle on their comrades who had been badly wounded by the creatures. That would heal the lacerations from their great claws, and the knights would be able to stand again. Thanks to the Miracle, they had somehow been holding the line against the monsters.

But the Miracle was not a true panacea. It would have no effect on the dead.

Many knights had died instantly from the creatures' attacks. The number of knights was slowly decreasing. Besides, even this all-powerful miracle drug couldn't heal wounds in an instant. It took a few minutes for the knights to return to combat, though this depended on the degree of injury. It was only a matter of time before the lines of battle crumbled.

As this fierce fight was going on, Brunhild saw the grotesque lion-creature that held Kriemhild in its jaws run away.

It was certain that the goal of this attack had been the kidnapping of the royal sisters.

Brunhild started running after Kriemhild. But the moment she did, someone scooped her up in their arms.

It was a knight who had survived the surprise attack. The knight was astride a horse and had pulled Brunhild up onto horseback.

Another knight, who was still fighting, cried to the knight astride the horse, "Take Princess Brunhild to the castle!"

Immediately after yelling that, said knight was killed by a creature.

Holding the princess in his arms, the knight on horseback commanded his horse into a gallop.

Brunhild ordered the knight, "Save Kriemhild!"

But the knight did not direct his horse toward Kriemhild.

"Please forgive me, Princess Brunhild." The knight muttered as if he was telling himself, "I'll only protect you…"

The knight's judgment was correct. The creatures from the foreign land were too strong, and the guard was half destroyed. They weren't equipped to make a recovery. So then there was nothing left but to flee. Rather than having both princesses carried off, it would be better to keep one safe.

Right before parting ways, the sisters' gazes met.

The younger sister, held in the lion's mouth and getting farther away, kept looking at Brunhild the whole time.

Her cries grew quiet and then ceased.

The lion-creature descended the mountain. It ran off in the opposite direction from the city. Judging from the surrounding scenery, Kriemhild figured it was running for the gates at the country's border.

As the lion ran along the grasslands with her in its mouth, the other attackers, also riding creatures, caught up to them. She could hear their conversation.

"Ha-ha! We've gotten 'God's Power.'"

"With research into this power, our country's military will make dramatic leaps."

So that was it after all. Just as her sister had said, it seemed she had been kidnapped to be used as an experimental animal.

Kriemhild was so frightened, she couldn't speak.

She could hear the voices of her attackers.

"But anyway, what an aggravating face on this girl."

"The more I look at her, the more she looks just like that queen."

In the past, these attackers had fought with the Fifth Queen—Kriemhild and Brunhild's mother—and lost. They held a particularly vicious animosity toward her.

"Let's have a little fun."

One of the attackers gave an order to the lion-creature. Instantly, the creature bit Kriemhild particularly hard.

"Ah…"

The vivid pain made Kriemhild cry out sharply. In those great jaws, even an adult wouldn't stand a chance, never mind a child.

But Kriemhild was safe. She wasn't bleeding. She wasn't even wounded.

"Hn…hnnnn…"

But she groaned from the pain that surged through her body.

The queens in every generation had had invincible bodies. The blessings of the Power of God within them kept ordinary weapons from injuring them. Brunhild and Kriemhild had both inherited the Power of God from their mother. However, the power must have waned with each successive generation, as they had only received that factor in part.

To be precise, the sisters' bodies were indestructible, but they could still get hurt.

If they were bitten, or if they were sliced, they would be wounded for a time and hurt. But then their partial Power of God would take effect and instantly heal their wounds. So they would ultimately be unwounded and invincible. The blessings the pair received from the Power of God had diminished, reduced from ironclad protection to a tenacious regenerative power.

When the carriage had overturned and Brunhild had protected Kriemhild, it had not been to protect her sister from injury, but to protect her sister from the pain.

They *did* feel pain. This was the troublesome part.

Seeing Kriemhild in pain, the attackers grinned. "Ha-ha! How pathetic!"

Being tormented made fear swell inside her.

What would happen to her after she was taken away? The fact that her body couldn't die only made her fear greater. Even if she were cut up, she could not die. She could not escape to death.

"S…Sis…ter…"

Kriemhild cried from fear. But there was no one to save her.

The creatures were as fast as horses, and once the knight who had fled reached the castle to call for reinforcements, he would not make it in time to save Kriemhild. So the attackers made her cry out as they pleased. It was a nasty sort of sport.

Her cries of "Sister!" rang out.

The attackers laughed at her.

"Ha-ha, ha-ha-ha-ha-ha-ha-ha!"

They bellowed and guffawed.

But…

…then their laughter came to a sudden stop.

That very moment, Kriemhild's tiny body flew through the sky. She looked to see an arrow stuck in the leg of the lion-creature. The creature, which had been running, lost balance and tumbled to the ground.

Tossed out onto soft grass, Kriemhild heard hoofbeats.

A horse was racing up to them. It was a knight's horse. But it was not a knight riding it.

It was a princess.

It was Brunhild. Brunhild had knocked her knight guard off his horse and stolen it away.

Astride the horse, Brunhild bore a bow. She never missed a target with her arrows. She had polished her skills many times by going out hunting, a pastime of the royal family. Despite being a young girl, she could make good use of every muscle in her body to shoot a bow that was built for adult men.

As Brunhild was pulling her next arrow out of her quiver and readying to pursue, Kriemhild cried, "Sister, please don't come after me!"

Moments before, she'd wanted her sister's help. But now she was worried her sister would be caught. She couldn't have Brunhild meet the same fate.

The elder sister ignored her younger sister's cries and nocked a second arrow.

Then she released it.

With a twanging sound, the second arrow pierced the attacker. Despite firing from an unstable horseback position, the arrow soared in fine trajectory, drawn toward the attacker's forehead.

"You brat!"

With his allies defeated, the attacker gave instructions to the lion-creatures. The creatures attacked Brunhild. Brunhild skillfully controlled her horse to try to evade them, but she wouldn't make it in time.

"!"

One creature made a sudden leap and snapped at Brunhild's neck. It grappled with her, and Brunhild fell from her horse to be pressed to the grass.

Brunhild was highly athletic, but she wasn't strong enough to knock aside a creature more than twice her weight.

Kriemhild heard a wheezing sound. It was Brunhild's breathing. The creature was biting into Brunhild's throat with its great jaw. There was pressure on her respiratory tract, and she couldn't breathe. Though it didn't wound the princess, at this rate, oxygen would fail to reach her brain, and in a few seconds, she would lose consciousness.

It was evident she would be taken away along with Kriemhild.

Brunhild's hand, seen from beneath the body of the lion-creature, seemed to spasm.

"Ahh, Sister…" It looked to Kriemhild as if she were struggling for oxygen.

But that wasn't it.

Suddenly, something like light was manifested in her right hand. That light was God's weapon.

In this kingdom, it was called Thunder.

It was an attack that fired God's Power like lightning. The First Queen was said to have been skilled in this technique.

Brunhild shot an attack from her right hand to burn the creature.

While she had inherited the Power of God from her mother, she had never used Thunder before—not because she lacked the aptitude. The danger of the situation had shocked the slumbering Power of God into awakening.

The creature's head burned to nothing. Its headless body collapsed on top of Brunhild. The blood flowed like a waterfall from the wound, soaking the grassy field.

Brunhild rolled out from under the creature's corpse to knit Thunder once more in the fingers of her right hand, firing it at the attacker. The attacker had never imagined his powerful servant would be killed by a little girl, and he was wide open.

The arrow of light pierced the attacker's limbs. The remaining creatures attacked Brunhild regardless, but they were no longer any match for her. Brunhild knew how to use the Thunder now. In the face of her arrows of light, the creatures died helplessly.

Sitting on the grassy field, Kriemhild watched her sister's heroism in a daze.

Once the battle was over, Brunhild came to her sister. Her pretty dress was filthy with mud and blood.

The elder sister called to her gently, "Are you hurt? ...Oh, I suppose not."

Kriemhild burst into immediate tears. "Hwahhhh! Ahhhhh!"

Now she wasn't crying from fear. She had burst into tears from relief. "Sister...Sister!" Because she was bawling, it was difficult to understand what she was saying. "Why...why were you so reckless...?"

Those words made Brunhild still. She looked at the bow lying beside her—the bow she'd stolen from the knight.

"You knew you couldn't win just with that," said Kriemhild.

"You're right. If I hadn't gotten lucky and become able to use the Thunder, then I would have been kidnapped, too."

"So then why...?"

"Because I was okay with that. It was better than letting them take you off to some scary place alone."

"You mustn't be like that, Sister. Please, never do something like this ever again..."

With an awkward look on her face, Brunhild said, "I don't know... if another villain appears...I think I'll go save you. No matter where you are."

"You can't do that, okay?!" But despite saying that, Kriemhild was so hopelessly glad of her sister's concern.

"Let's go back. The knights will be worried." Brunhild took Kriemhild's hand and brought her to the horse she'd been riding.

The pair got on the horse and galloped back to the castle.

Brunhild rode in front, with Kriemhild behind her.

Kriemhild wrapped her arms around her sister's waist to keep from falling off the horse.

She could feel her sister's body heat through her back.

It was warm.

* * *

Two years passed after that, and one day, when the elder sister was fifteen and the younger had turned fourteen, something happened.

Their mother, the reigning queen, fell ill.

It was because of the corrosion.

This was the fate of those of the Siegfried family. All of them would die young because of the Power of God they harbored in their bodies. They would become unable to bear this power, which was too much for the human body, and their flesh would break down. This was the fated "corrosion."

Currently, the queen was focused on treatment in the royal castle, but it was clear there was no expectation she would get better. The reigning queen was the fifth generation of queens. Thus far, the same fate had befallen four previous queens, and they had all died without being cured. This queen was basically as good as dead at this point.

And once the queen fell ill, there came the question of which of the two princesses would inherit the throne.

In order to discuss the matter of succession to the throne, Brunhild headed to Kriemhild's room.

Brunhild said to her sister, "The crowning ceremony will be one year from now. That will formally decide which of us will become queen…but, Kriemhild, I'm thinking I will be queen."

Kriemhild had no objections.

"I think that's a good idea. I lack your majesty, Sister. I'm not capable of standing above others."

"That's not the reason why… You're kind, Kriemhild. I think that's why you're not suited to standing in a position of authority."

Brunhild was worried. Her concern was that if her little sister were to become queen, then various parties would certainly try to take advantage of her kindness.

Kriemhild said to Brunhild, "I believe you will surely become the most amazing queen. Please make the kingdom an even better place than it is now."

"I'll do it. I don't know if I can manage everything perfectly like the First Queen, but I'll do what I…" Brunhild stopped there.

"Sister?"

"Ngh…"

Suddenly, Brunhild clutched her chest in pain. Her face turned pale, and she broke into a cold sweat that wouldn't stop. In the end, she fell to her knees on the carpet.

"Sister! Sister!"

It seemed like some kind of illness. Kriemhild panicked, but she pulled a little bottle out from her accessory case. Inside it was a golden liquid.

"It's all right, Sister. I've brought some of the Miracle of Life."

Of the great feats accomplished by the First Queen, the Miracle of Life was particularly outstanding.

The First Queen had been able to turn water she touched with her right hand into the Miracle. The effects of the Miracle were tremendous, and it would drive away all illness and heal any injury. She had managed to transcend all except death.

Even after the death of the First Queen, the generations of queens had continued to make the Miracle. And the result of those efforts was that the Miracle had spread far and wide, and now, there was no more illness or injury in the kingdom.

"Sister, please open your mouth."

Brunhild opened her mouth like a little bird. Pouring the Miracle in, Kriemhild was relieved—since this would cure any illness.

But...

"Hah...hah...hahh...!"

Even though the Miracle should have taken effect a few minutes after swallowing, even after waiting about ten minutes, Brunhild's pain showed no sign of easing.

In the end, she even coughed up blood. The fresh blood dirtied the floor.

"No...why?" Though Kriemhild was quite rattled, she considered what she could do. "A doctor... I'll go call a doctor. Sister, please be patient."

Kriemhild left the room and went to call for a doctor.

But she couldn't find one right away. Since the panacea that was the Miracle of Life had spread throughout the country, the profession of doctor had largely perished. The court physician who had once been at the royal villa had been relieved of his post quite some time ago.

In the end, it took one full night before a doctor came, since they had no choice but to bring in the doctor who attended the queen from the royal palace.

On seeing Brunhild's state, the queen's attending doctor said, "This is the same as Her Majesty. No—it's even worse."

According to the doctor, the Power of God in Brunhild's body had already begun to affect her adversely.

"This is, without question, the corrosion."

The corrosion could not be cured even with the Miracle of Life because both of them originated from the Power of God, which was of the same type.

While watching her sleeping sister, Kriemhild asked the doctor, "My sister…what will become of her?"

"Her body will weaken. With her health like this, it seems unlikely she will succeed the throne…"

The doctor's judgment was correct.

Day by day, Brunhild grew weaker.

First, she lost her endurance. Just a little movement would leave her out of breath. Even though she had been athletic, her muscles simply wasted away. Her skin began to grow pale. Her eyes grew sunken. She coughed, then spat blood.

Eventually, the color of her hair and eyes changed.

Her hair became white, and her eyes red.

Brunhild's natural colors had begun to wane.

She became a sickly, pale princess.

As Brunhild weakened, the courtiers began to give up on her.

"There is no longer any chance Princess Brunhild will succeed the throne."

"So then it's a waste of time to serve her."

With such remarks, all the courtiers distanced themselves from Brunhild.

One night, Kriemhild visited her sister's room.

When Brunhild, lying in bed, saw Kriemhild, she smiled weakly, then coughed. "I'm glad you've come."

The chamberlain and the others didn't involve themselves with

Brunhild more than necessary. That had to be due to their discomfort around someone with an incurable illness.

"Just a little while ago, there were so many subjects trying to curry favor with me, but even they have come to ignore me. And once they're all gone, it does get lonely," said Brunhild.

"Even if all your retainers abandon you, I shall stay by your side. And so," Kriemhild went on, "please give up on becoming queen. I know you still haven't given up on the throne, and that you've been pushing yourself when you're ill, studying diligently in order to become queen."

Secretly, Brunhild had been continuing the cultural studies necessary to become queen and struggling to regain her health—all while ignoring the backbiting from the courtiers.

"Right now, the best thing you can do is to care for your health," said Kriemhild.

"But...if I don't become queen, then that means you'll ascend the throne."

"I don't mind. I'm sure I wouldn't be as reliable as you, but I will fulfill my duties. So please, rest."

"I cannot heed that request."

"Why...?"

Brunhild got a faraway look in her eyes.

It was a mysterious look, as if she were looking somewhere that was not here. "...I've come to understand something, from being struck by the corrosion. It seems the Power of God has affected my eyes, and they have become more like those of the Divine. I can see the future—though only vaguely." Her gaze shifted to Kriemhild. "You must not become queen. You will surely meet a cruel fate."

"A cruel fate..."

"Though I don't know specifically what will happen." Brunhild drew her sister to her in an embrace in attempt to reassure her. "Don't worry. I'll protect you. I always have, haven't I?"

"Yes, I do feel better..."

That was a lie.

Brunhild's embrace was so weak, it just made Kriemhild even more anxious.

* * *

Brunhild stepped out of bed and began working of her own accord.

The situation wouldn't change if she just lay in bed. The doctor had given up on treating her condition.

Leaving the royal castle, Brunhild headed for the Academy.

The Academy was a large research institution that gathered scholars, domestic and foreign. After being freed from the control of the evil dragons, the kingdom had built this facility in order to facilitate exchange with other nations. The First Queen had been the one to establish it. The goal of the kingdom was to invite scholars from abroad and to adopt technologies their own nation lacked. The scholars from foreign lands came in order to learn about technology and scholarship that existed only in their kingdom—mainly about spirits and magic.

She thought that there, she might be able to find some clue to healing the corrosion. The study of medicine and pharmacy had declined in the kingdom due to its reliance on the Miracle, so the only place she could learn those things was the Academy, which had knowledge exchange with foreign countries.

Upon arriving at the Academy, Brunhild suddenly said to the dean, "Prepare a research room for my exclusive use. Make it so I can stay the night there and study."

The dean was troubled. "All of the rooms in the Academy are being used to various purposes. I'm very sorry, but there are no rooms that you might use…"

"The basement is free, isn't it?"

"What?!" The dean was shocked. "But underneath this academy…"

"I know. I don't mind. Don't worry—I'm the daughter of the dragonslayer."

"If you say so, Your Highness."

The basement was cleaned out at once and made Brunhild's exclusive room.

In that underground research lab, Brunhild began researching the corrosion.

Once she finished her first day of research and sat down in the bed to sleep—

—that thing in the basement appeared before her.

<I never thought I would have a visitor on waking from my sleep.>

It was not a human's voice she heard. It was a mysterious voice that rang in her mind.

This was the language called the "Dragon's Tongue."

So the owner of that voice was a dragon.

Appearing from the depths of the underground room was a dragon eight meters long and over five meters high. He had amber scales and eyes.

Brunhild was not surprised to see the dragon.

She had known there was a dragon in the basement. That was the reason she had chosen this place.

Once, many dragons had lurked in this kingdom.

This amber dragon was one of the survivors.

Until one hundred years ago, this kingdom had been under the control of an evil dragon, and dragons that were his private army had been stationed all over the land. But the dragons who had been his soldiers had not been dragons from birth. They had originally been humans but had had their free will stolen from them and had been transformed into dragons through the evil dragon's sorcery.

Those dragons had all been exterminated by the queen, but some very few dragons had been spared. Those dragons who had miraculously maintained their awareness as humans had not been killed. They appeared to be dragons in likeness, but their hearts remained human. Even so, dragons could not be let out into the world. The kingdom was a place where dragons had brought about tragedy countless times. As a result, they had dealt with the issue by locking them away in basements or prison towers.

Brunhild gazed at the dragon. There was no fear in her eyes, surprising him.

<You don't fear, even before a dragon?>

Brunhild said to the dragon, <We're going to be living together starting today, so best regards. Relax. I will not interfere with your lifestyle.>

<So you can use the Dragon's Tongue? You must be a dragonslaying princess.>

<That I am. I'm a princess of the Siegfried family.>

Those who could speak the Dragon's Tongue appeared frequently in the bloodline of the Siegfried family. Brunhild and Kriemhild both could.

The Dragon's Tongue did not need to be spoken out loud. They were able to say what they thought into the mind of another without any accompanying sound.

The amber dragon gazed fixedly at her, then muttered as if deeply moved, <I see, the First's...> There was affection in his eyes as he looked at her.

While getting into bed, Brunhild said, <Then I'm going to sleep for the night. Oh, if you want to attack me, then go right ahead.>

<Why would I attack you? Against the dragonslayer's daughter, a dragon has no chance of winning.>

She'd joked about it because she knew she was invincible to a dragon.

The next morning, as soon as Brunhild woke up, she began her research. The amber dragon watched her closely as she did.

The dragon did not try to interfere with the princess.

Having said she would not interfere with his lifestyle, she didn't speak to him, either.

Three days passed since her coming.

During these three days, the amber dragon didn't speak to her and just watched her.

Brunhild grew impatient with this. She said, <...If you have something to say, then could you say it?>

The dragon answered, <I cannot bother you when you're focused on your research.>

<It's distracting when you keep watching me like that.> She returned the book she had in hand to the bookshelf and walked to the dragon. Then she brought her face close to the dragon's and said, <Is it so much fun to watch me?>

<It is fun,> the dragon answered without hesitation. <I've been locked underground for nearly a hundred years. Nobody has come to visit me, and I've never gone outside. And in my boredom, you appeared to me. Every single ordinary gesture of yours is exciting to me. And you're also a fair woman—so of course I would not tire of watching you.>

<Oh, dear...> A tinge of pink colored Brunhild's cheeks. <I'd

heard that dragons were noble creatures and wouldn't attempt to seduce women.>

<I am not a pure dragon. I was originally human. I will certainly make a move to seduce a pretty lady.>

The dragon said, <I should ask you why you're locking yourself up in this basement. The life of a flower is brief. You should see the light of the sun and have fun with men.>

<I'm a little tired. And involving myself with men...>

Brunhild told him what had brought her to this research lab.

She told him that she was a princess, that she was supposed to have ascended to the throne but had given up on that due to the corrosion, and that as soon as her chances of succeeding the throne had evaporated, the people around her had begun to abandon her.

<So I think this is perfect—a basement with a dragon locked away... I wanted to be away from people.>

<Unfortunately, I am a human in the shape of a dragon. I'm sure the dragons you seek are only in the Eden paradises.>

Brunhild hung her head and said, <Yes, I'm sure that's true.>

Perhaps since she looked a little lonely, the dragon showed consideration and continued, <...Well, though I am originally human, I've been away from the world for a long time. I have no interest in human status or money. Whether you become queen or not, it doesn't matter to me. I could well imitate the sort of noble dragon you wish for.>

Brunhild broke into titters. <Is there any point to nobility if I know it is imitated?>

<I wouldn't know, either.>

She said, <But that being the case, it seems you wouldn't turn your back on me.>

<I would not. You are the first person I've had to talk to in a hundred years, after all.>

<Amber Dragon, what is your name?>

The dragon called himself Bernstein. It had been his name when he'd been human.

After that, Brunhild and Bernstein came to chat about various things.

Brunhild often talked about her sister. No matter what subject she brought up, it almost always was related to her sister. Bernstein could tell just how much she cared for her.

<In order to save my sister, I must become queen. And cure the corrosion...>

Bernstein thought he would help her with her research. He was quite touched by her sisterly love.

Besides, Bernstein had a debt of gratitude toward the First Queen. Once, he had just about been killed by a dragonslayer. His opponent had been a boy dragonslayer. The one to save Bernstein's life when he had been in this predicament had been none other than the First Queen herself.

And the grandchild of that First Queen was in trouble. He had to help.

<I will share with you my blood and scales. The blood of a dragon is a deadly poison, but if you dilute it, it becomes a medicine. And if my scales are decocted, they can make a medicine as well.>

Brunhild was very grateful to receive Bernstein's proposal. There were still many mysterious effects of dragon blood and scales that had yet to be understood.

<Thank you, Bernstein.>

Through a process of continual trial and error, Brunhild made a medicine to cure the corrosion.

One year passed, and having spent all her time in research, the princess turned sixteen.

The trial drug to cure the corrosion was finally complete.

But the time limit was also nigh.

Approaching in three days was the day to decide the official successor to the throne.

Brunhild held the completed trial drug in shaking hands. <If this doesn't work, then I...>

To encourage her, Bernstein said, <Of course it will work. You've spent this whole past year on this medicine.>

Brunhild smiled weakly. <That remark isn't even consolation...>

<It's not meant as consolation. I've seen your efforts this past year. But if you say you will not drink it, then I'd still stand to

benefit. Since once you cure the corrosion, that means you'll stop coming to this basement.> Bernstein did indeed feel like he didn't want to lose his only conversation partner. <I think you need not drink it, if you want to always be with me.>

<I don't want to be with you always...but once I'm cured, I could come see you sometimes.>

Then she steeled herself and drank down the trial drug.

Bernstein thought that this was for the best.

Now there was only to wait for the drug to work. This drug that was the culmination of a year's worth of effort...

But...

Brunhild coughed. When she pressed a hand against her mouth, there was blood on it.

The drug had not worked.

Brunhild was filled with despair.

She wound up sitting on a chair in the basement, dazedly staring into the corner. She no longer worked at the research she had been so passionate about. The experimental tools and half-read books lying on her desk were lonely.

No matter what Bernstein said to her, it was no use. Like a doll, she didn't say a word. He couldn't even think of what to say to her in the first place. He had seen her efforts over the past year. And they had all come to nothing.

Three days passed, and finally, Brunhild opened her mouth. "I'm sorry, Kriemhild. I'm making you be queen..."

Brunhild figured this was his chance to cheer her up. <Brunhild. How about you try living for yourself this time? You could make a drug to cure the corrosion or enjoy the rest of your life. At the very least, that would be better than locking yourself up in this dark basement.>

Brunhild answered, <I should say that of you.>

<Of me?>

Brunhild pulled a gem out of the pocket of her dress. It was a sapphire necklace, with ancient characters carved on the gem.

She put it around the dragon's neck.

Then she closed her eyes.

Suddenly, Bernstein's body began to glow.

The shining dragon silhouette turned into the shape of a human.
"What...?"

By the time the light vanished, Bernstein had become human. It was his own body, which he'd lost long ago.

Looking at himself reflected in the mirror to the side, Bernstein patted at his own cheeks.

"Among dragons' spells, there is one that turns them into human form. It seems you didn't know because you're not a pure dragon, though. I read a dragon's book that was in my childhood home, and I tried carving that spell into a gem."

The sapphire sparkled at Bernstein's neck.

"I actually planned to leave this basement together with you—I having cured the corrosion, and you as a human again. But my part never worked out...," she said with her eyes closed, voice trembling. Tears seeped out from her shut eyelids. She had closed her eyes to hold back the tears, but it was no use.

That brought Bernstein to the verge of tears as well. It had been a very long time since he'd felt this sensation of welling tears. Since dragons weren't made to shed tears, it had been nearly a century since he'd felt he would cry. No matter what sorrow he'd felt from his isolation, his eyes hadn't even watered.

"Now go, Bernstein. You can go anywhere now."

"Of course I can't go," Bernstein answered her in a human voice.

This was the girl who had gotten him back his human body. If he were to leave her behind, then he could never enjoy himself no matter where he went, and he also thought that would not be the act of a human.

"Brunhild—you are a princess. Make me your servant. I want to support you until your life comes to an end."

Brunhild smiled wryly. "Are you quite serious?"

"I'm not a fan of poor jokes."

"What a man of strange tastes... Well, so be it. Your job won't last long anyway."

And so the dragon became Brunhild's servant.

"I swear I will be useful to you," he said.

"Then my best regards once more, Bernstei...n..."

Brunhild's eyes had been closed all this time, and now she slowly opened them. Seeing Bernstein, she was struck speechless.

She went red to her ears and hung her head. She looked away.

Because Bernstein was entirely naked.

It was obvious, if you thought about it. Dragons didn't wear clothing. So if he returned to human form, of course he wouldn't be wearing clothing.

"Th-this is the first I've seen a gentleman in the nude…"

With his muscular physique, like a sculpture, before her, Brunhild's mind went completely blank.

"For now, I'll go borrow some scholar's clothes for you…"

The two of them left the Academy together.

Brunhild deliberately went the long way around to walk the way to the royal villa. She did this out of consideration for Bernstein, who would be walking in town for the first time in a hundred years.

Now human again, Bernstein was a man in his mid-twenties. His characteristic feature was his cool, almond eyes. His features were indeed handsome; he was the type women wouldn't leave alone. Brunhild remembered when they'd first met, and they'd talked about whether he would try to seduce her or not.

"But the town is unsurprisingly completely different after a hundred years."

The way he looked all around him was just like how a boy might.

It's his first time out in a century. It's no surprise…

But his eyes were sparkling. She found it quite charming.

"There's a restaurant there. I'd love to stop by." Bernstein pointed at a place with meat dishes.

Brunhild was just in the mood for meat as well. Since she'd been cooped up so long, her body wanted something to invigorate it. "Yes, let's go."

They went into the restaurant, and the two of them ordered plenty of meat dishes.

As Bernstein was practically pouring food down his throat, Brunhild asked him, "You don't resent humans?"

Bernstein tilted his head. "Why would I?"

"I mean, wouldn't you? Since just because you looked like a dragon, you were locked up underground for a very long time."

"That's true. I am angry." But despite saying that, there wasn't a shred of anger in his tone. He seemed rather detached from it. "What happened to me one hundred years ago was discrimination. No matter what I said...though they had no hope of understanding... people wouldn't listen to me and tried to kill me."

"So then..."

"But one hundred years ago, I was blessed with love—the love of your ancestor, the First. She was the one person who protected me and gave me shelter. Until she passed away, I lived in the royal castle. Though in terms of time, it was but a few years."

Bernstein had a gentle look in his eyes. "I remember quite well the view from the royal castle. I know the town it overlooked was full of humans who discriminated against me, but it was still beautiful."

"Since it was the country built by the woman you respected and loved."

"That was part of it."

"So then," Brunhild said, sounding a little weak, "you may not like the country the way it is now. The queens have just been in decline since the time of the First. And this country as well."

Attacks from foreign nations had increased, and there were signs that discrimination had returned.

Dissatisfaction with their ruler had hardened the hearts of the people.

"You might have been happier to remain in that basement."

"But," Bernstein said. "I love this country not only because it's the nation the First built. I love people to begin with. They are foolish, but that's what makes them dear."

Dear because they were foolish. Hearing that, Brunhild said frankly, "I don't really understand."

Bernstein smiled. "I appreciate your honesty. If you were to say you understand, at your age, it would be a lie. If you get older, the time may come when you understand."

"Is that how it is?"

"That's how it is."

Bernstein looked out the window at the town and said, "So this country is still beautiful—even changed as it is, since that's the proof that the people are alive."

As he said that, he looked to Brunhild like a noble dragon—

even though right now, he was human once more from the power of the gem.

Finishing their meal, the two of them headed for the royal villa.

Brunhild realized she was in a good mood for the first time in quite a while—as she also realized that she had been quite constantly miserable lately.

"Thank you, Bernstein."

"Whatever for?"

"Walking through the town with you seems to have cheered me up a little."

"You need not thank me. I simply wished to walk through the town with a becoming maiden."

If only he could do something about that flippant attitude, Brunhild thought with a wry smile.

Kriemhild had always felt like she was good for nothing.

She lacked her sister's acumen; she was timid and not very cheerful. What she hated the most was that she was always being saved by her sister.

She had always felt that just once, she wanted to help Brunhild.

And then her sister had fallen ill with the corrosion.

If she was to help Brunhild, then now was the only time. Kriemhild made use of all her authority as a princess to search for a way to heal her. As people saw her as likely to become the next queen, many vassals around her would do what she said. In all honesty, she didn't want to rely on people with such ulterior motives, but she did anyway, thinking it might help her sister.

She searched not only within the country, but also sought a way to heal her sister abroad.

But in the end, she couldn't find a single cure.

That night, with the coronation ceremony two days away, her sister returned to the royal villa. For this past year, she had been at the Academy researching a way to cure the corrosion, but it seemed her attempts there had not gone well. Kriemhild was disappointed in herself, wishing she could have found a cure to welcome her sister with.

And then something happened right at the same time Brunhild and Bernstein were having lunch together.

As Kriemhild was wallowing in self-loathing, a man arrived.

The man's name was Warren.

"Pardon me, Princess," he said, and came into Kriemhild's quarters.

Warren was an old retainer of the royal family. He had served continuously from the time of the First Queen until the current queen, the Fifth. Even given that the queens of successive generations had been short-lived, Warren had to be over ninety years old, as a conservative estimate. However, he looked young for his age and could even pass for being in his fifties. His spine was straight, and he was tall. There were deep wrinkles in the corners of his eyes and between his brows. His gaze was as sharp as a hawk's.

Surprised by his sudden visit, Kriemhild asked, "Warren, what brings you to the royal villa?"

Warren was the chief vassal and an aide to the queen. She had heard that he had continued to serve without leaving for even a moment since the Fifth Queen had ascended to the throne. For him to leave his queen on her sickbed and come to the royal villa felt strange to Kriemhild.

"I have something to give you." From beneath the long coat he wore, Warren produced a sword. He drew it from its sheath. The beautiful blade sparkled enticingly. "It's called the Healing Blade. It is not a sword for hurting people. It is a sword for healing. The foreign spells cast on it dispel magic and ease the ailments of its owner."

This sounded like a strange tale, but Kriemhild thought, *I see.* The warm coloring of this sword's blade was convincing and made her believe it really did have healing spells cast on it.

Warren sheathed the sword and offered it to Kriemhild.

"The queens of each generation have all carried this sword. This healing even has a rare effect on the corrosion. Without this sword, any queen would have passed away before seeing age thirty. I've come with orders from Her Majesty the Queen to deliver this to you."

"Why me? If this sword has an effect against the corrosion, then my mother should be the one to keep it."

"This sword will heal the symptoms of the corrosion, but it cannot cure it. Her Majesty has judged that there is no longer any point to her keeping the sword. As the queen's successor, the next wielder should be you, Kriemhild."

Kriemhild took the sword.

Perhaps this was in her head, but she felt as if she could sense her mother's warm heart in the blade.

"Mother…" Ever quick to cry, Kriemhild could feel the tears welling up but forced them back down. Ever since she'd decided she didn't want to be weak anymore, she had forbidden herself from crying.

"I also wish for you to live as long as possible, Your Highness." Warren continued, "And I hope that you would serve the kingdom as long as possible. With all due respect, that is the duty of a queen… To protect the honor of the kingdom, as it was. That is my wish, as a man who has continued to serve successive generations of queens."

Kriemhild answered quite sincerely, "I will do everything that I can."

Hearing that, Warren turned his back to Kriemhild. It seemed he had finished his business.

As he was about to leave the room, Kriemhild said, "Thank you, Warren."

Warren paused there for a moment but then left the room without looking back.

Once it was night, Brunhild returned to the royal villa.

Kriemhild immediately headed to Brunhild's chambers.

"Welcome back, Sister."

When Kriemhild came into her quarters, Brunhild welcomed her. "I'm back. I was just thinking to go see you." Then she hung her head and said, "…I'm sorry. I never did manage to heal the corrosion in the end."

"You need not apologize for that, Sister. I've prepared myself to become queen in my own way… I should be the one to apologize. I wasn't able to do anything to help you."

Kriemhild had no knowledge of pharmacy, and she had spent this past year training in various subjects so as to become the next queen. For this past year, the sisters hadn't really seen each other.

Brunhild gazed at Kriemhild. Her eyes were distant, just like they had been some time ago, as if she were gazing somewhere else. Her eyes could see the future where Kriemhild became queen—and that it was not a very good one.

Noticing that look, Kriemhild said, "Sister. Please don't look at me with such concern. I'm already fifteen. I'm not only your little sister, constantly needing your protection."

"But…"

"Do you lack trust in me so? Please believe in me—I'm your sister." Kriemhild's tone was unusually forceful, for her.

Kriemhild had made up her mind on this while Brunhild had been immersed in her research.

She would no longer cause her sister to worry.

Her kind sister would constantly worry about her, even when her own life was in danger. While that made her glad, even more than that, it brought her sorrow.

It was time for her to be independent.

The younger sister's eyes, looking upon her elder, were brimming with strong determination. From that, Brunhild understood—as she had been busy elsewhere, her sister had become stronger.

It was reassuring enough, and it made her want to believe in her younger sister.

"I believe in you, Kriemhild. Show me that you will drive away the dark future I see."

"Yes. I will. And this time, I will save you." Kriemhild continued, "Now, once I become queen, there are things I want to do. Once I can direct the knights of the kingdom at my will, I want to conquer Eden. Since the fruit of knowledge that grows there will surely be able to cure your corrosion."

"Kriemhild…"

Two days after that, Kriemhild's coronation ceremony came.

That morning, Kriemhild left the royal villa.

That was where the two of them had lived all their lives. The villa had been built quite some time ago, and all princesses were only allowed to live there. Only the queen was allowed to live at the royal castle.

Before Kriemhild left the royal villa, Brunhild came to the gates to see her off. That gladdened Kriemhild.

"Please take care of our mother, ill at the castle—enough for my part as well," said Brunhild.

"Yes. I'll tell her you're worried for her."

All this time, the two sisters had not been able to visit their mother even once. Her health must have been quite poor, as visits had been forbidden. Although the two of them had had hardly any contact with their mother since they had been small, so being unable to see her was nothing new.

Brunhild kissed Kriemhild's forehead, and she prayed for her younger sister's new life. "I pray that your reign be a bright one."

Kriemhild returned her kiss.

"Sister, there's something I want to give you." She drew something out and gave it to her elder sister.

It was the Healing Blade.

"This is for you. It is not a sword for taking lives. It's a sword that protects life. It's said to drive away evil and protect its owner. While I doubt it can cure your corrosion, I think it should ease your suffering."

Brunhild's eyes widened. "Amazing. Even just with a glance, I can tell it's a miraculous object." She accepted the sword and hugged it to her chest. "Thank you. I will carry it with me always."

"Please do. It seems you must carry it for it to take effect."

"How did you acquire it?"

Kriemhild smiled and answered, "A servant dispatched to a foreign land obtained it."

That was a lie. She couldn't possibly be honest about how she had acquired it. If she spoke of how the queens of successive generations had struggled against the corrosion with help from that sword, then her sister would never accept the blade. Obviously, she would say that Kriemhild should carry it for her health.

Kriemhild's heart ached a little. She had lied to her sister and also betrayed her mother, who had gifted her with the sword, as well as Warren, who had said he wanted her to live a long life. Kriemhild herself was conflicted about whether to give this sword to her sister, too. Her struggle was not over how her own life might shorten by giving it away. It was about betraying the goodwill toward her. For the whole two days until the coronation ceremony was to be held, Kriemhild had agonized over it, and then she had somehow managed to resolve herself to hand the sword to her sister.

From Kriemhild's waist hung a sword that much resembled the Healing Blade. She had asked a big favor of the greatest blacksmith in the land, having him make this fake sword in two days. It was to fool her mother and Warren once she reached the royal castle.

Out of guilt, Kriemhild partially confessed, "…I've done something a little bad in order to give you that sword."

Brunhild was surprised. She didn't know what sort of bad thing Kriemhild had done, but she hadn't imagined the words "I've done something bad" would ever come from her sister's mouth.

With upturned eyes, as if examining her sister's reaction, Kriemhild said, "Please forgive me—it was a deed done because I want you to get well, no matter what."

Unable to bear it, Brunhild embraced her sister hard. "How can you be so adorable when you're going to become queen today?"

Brunhild didn't let go of Kriemhild for a long time.

After a lengthy embrace, Kriemhild was finally able to head for the royal castle.

In a room of the royal castle, the old retainer Warren was awaiting Kriemhild's coming.

In his hands was a dark-gray crown.

During the coronation, Warren would carry out the crowning himself.

Warren gazed closely at the crown in his hands. And then he murmured in the silence, "Your Majesty, the First."

Eventually, a knight came to Warren's room and reported, "Princess Kriemhild has arrived."

With the crown in his hands, Warren headed to the throne room.

After that, the coronation ceremony was held.

Kriemhild became the queen.

Two weeks had passed since Kriemhild had moved into the royal castle.

During that time, Kriemhild had not sent any correspondence to Brunhild at all. Neither had Brunhild interfered with Kriemhild's business. She figured that she would be quite overwhelmed with the unfamiliar duties of a queen.

One night, Brunhild was lying on her back in her bed in her quarters. At her side was the sword she had received from her sister. She

slept with her arms around it every night, as if it were a replacement for her sister. Thanks to that, these past few days, Brunhild's health had improved quite magnificently. By keeping the sword on her at all times, the blade's healing power had manifested to the utmost extent.

"Your Highness," came a call with a knock.

"Come in," she replied. From the voice, she could tell who had come.

Opening the door to come in was Bernstein, dressed in a waiter's clothes. Since regaining his human form, he had come to care for Brunhild's daily needs as her servant. He was pushing a silver cart with food atop it.

"I've brought you your dinner, Your Highness," Bernstein said to Brunhild, speaking more formally now that he was her chamberlain.

"You don't have to speak that way when we're alone. I just can't get used to it."

During the time they had spent together in the basement, Bernstein hadn't spoken formally with Brunhild. Even if he was her chamberlain now, having him be so formal to her just didn't sit right.

"All right, then I won't."

Bernstein placed the food atop the table.

Seeing all the food, Brunhild was disappointed.

It was nothing but things thought to be good for one's health, mainly fruit and vegetables.

"Do I have to eat it…?" Brunhild ate an unbalanced diet. "I'm not going to die even if I don't eat it anyhow."

Being protected by the Power of God, she would not die of starvation. The only thing that could kill her was the corrosion.

"Just eat it." Bernstein continued to set the food on the table, not listening to what she had to say at all.

Bernstein wanted Brunhild to be healthy. He didn't know how much effect fruit and vegetables would ultimately have on the corrosion, but still, there was the chance it could improve her health a little, so he figured he would try.

Brunhild also understood that, more or less. "…Oh well. I'll eat it, for you," she said.

She hated fruit and vegetables. But she did like Bernstein's consideration.

If I'd had a father, I wonder if he would have been kind to me like this.

Bernstein scooped up some fruit yogurt with a silver spoon and proffered it before Brunhild's mouth. He meant that she should open her mouth.

Brunhild obediently opened her lips.

That was when she realized something—it seemed she was behaving a little childishly dependent around Bernstein.

With both of her parents out of the picture, she'd had to protect her little sister. She had grown up self-disciplined, telling herself she had to be a reliable person. So ever since she was young, she had been unable to act like a child. But now, the situation had changed a little.

It felt easy to rely on Bernstein, and it was comfortable.

Around the time when Brunhild had finished her meal, someone bearing a longsword came before the gates of the royal villa.

The sentry noticed that person and, with spear in hand, called them to a halt. "Wait. Who do you serve?"

The night sky was cloudy, and the sentry couldn't see the visitor's face properly.

There was a slight break in the clouds. The moonlight, shining between the clouds, lit the face of the sword-bearer.

"P-pardon me!"

The sentry apologized and straightened his posture.

But that person must have been very displeased by the sentry's attitude.

They drew their longsword.

The blade flashed like lightning running through the dead of night.

The sentry was cut down and fell. A smell like sizzling flesh rose up.

That person bore a sword glowing golden. It was a blade that could even burn through armor.

While the other sentries were shocked, they raised their weapons.

"Have you gone mad, Your—?"

The golden sword soundlessly cut down the sentries, one after another. Nearly ten trained sentries rushed to the fight, but none of them even managed to wound the visitor.

The visitor slew all the soldiers who came—

—and then stepped into the royal villa.

* * *

There was clamoring within the villa. Brunhild and Bernstein could hear the noise as well.

"What is going on…?"

She was alerted to the commotion right as there was a bang on the door.

The one to enter was the villa's elderly butler. "Princess Brunhild… please flee… An attack…"

After getting that far, the elderly butler collapsed on his face. There was a deep slice on his back. By the time Brunhild approached, the old man had already passed away.

Bernstein was puzzled. "An attack?"

"Foreigners may have come to kidnap the princess. This happened a few years ago as well."

"So then shall we escape out the window?"

"No, we fight."

This was different from the time they had been attacked a few years ago. Now Brunhild had the power to fight. She was not so attached to the people of the royal villa, but neither did she want to see them thoughtlessly killed. With her sword at her hip, Brunhild stood from the table.

"I shall help."

Bernstein's body glowed. A moment later, he had become an amber dragon. He had become able to independently control the effect of the necklace he had received from Brunhild. So long as he wore it, he could freely become human or dragon.

The crackle of lightning ran through the fingers of Brunhild's right hand, like a warm-up.

She couldn't be killed, and she had a weapon that could even kill a dragon. On top of that, she had her dragon servant.

The attackers had no chance of winning.

The princess and dragon kept a watchful eye out around them as they walked the corridor of the royal villa.

Here and there, she saw the bodies of those who served her. There were countless bodies not only of soldiers, but also of servants. But it was concerning that there were no bodies of any attackers at all. If they could avoid making a single sacrifice when up against trained soldiers, then they had to be an extremely expert group.

As they came closer to the sounds of fighting, a burnt smell began to waft around.

They reached the main hall. There were little fires here and there. Wooden desks and chairs were burning.

And there was someone who looked like an attacker. They were right in the middle of cutting down a soldier.

The attacker's back was turned to them. Their face couldn't be seen.

But she could check who it was after they defeated them.

Brunhild threw the Thunder woven between her fingers at the attacker. Thunder was an effective weapon against dragons, but it also worked on humans. The high energy would burn the enemy.

When flung, Thunder would always kill and was impossible to dodge. The attacker's fate was sealed.

Or so it *should* have been.

While turning around, the attacker swung their sword. When the Thunder struck its blade, it was negated.

"What...?"

It was impossible.

No matter what a well-forged blade it was, it was impossible for a weapon made by human hands to negate Thunder.

The blade the figure had swung—it was shining the same color as Thunder.

Flames moved from the heated sword to the carpet and blazed up. In the blink of an eye, the main hall became a sea of fire.

In the ocean of red, a black silhouette appeared in just one spot.

It was a woman—seen from behind, she was terribly familiar.

"...It can't be," Brunhild murmured, her voice trembling violently. It was absurd. There was no way.

The attacker, turning around—

—had the same face as Brunhild's younger sister.

"Kriemhild...?"

"Sister...ah, I've finally found you."

Her voice was the same as Kriemhild's.

"Is that...Kriemhild?"

"Who else does it look like?"

She wasn't seeing things. The one there was without a doubt Kriemhild.

"Did...did you do this?" Brunhild asked, looking at the scattered corpses.

"Yes. Since they got in my way... But those are trivial matters and not important." She disregarded the deaths of the servants, casually treating them as "trivial matters."

"Sister, I've come with a request," Kriemhild said with hollow eyes. "Will you die?"

Brunhild was speechless. The woman before her just didn't seem like Kriemhild. There was no way her adorable little sister would tell her to die. Even if she had said that, there would be a reason.

"Kriemhild, what happened? Did something happen at the castle? Couldn't you tell me?"

"I went to the castle, and I became queen. And then I found out— about the responsibility of the queens of every generation. As a queen, I must also fulfill my responsibility. I need your life."

Longsword in hand, Kriemhild stepped forward. She moved so quickly, you would never imagine it was that same gentle Kriemhild.

Before swinging the sword, Kriemhild whispered.

Offer yourself to the kingdom.

Brunhild didn't move, because she was certain her sister would never hurt her.

That was why she was cut down.

She was slashed diagonally from the shoulder. Fresh blood spurted out. She could see beneath her eyes as her body opened up like a flower. That sight slowly flowed on by.

Brunhild understood that she had died.

Brunhild's body had received the favor of God—she couldn't be killed by a human weapon. But if it was a weapon made with the Power of God, then she *could* be killed. The golden sword Kriemhild bore was exactly that. Its attributes were the same as the Thunder Brunhild threw. Wounds made with this would not regenerate.

Her eyeballs moved, looking down at her body. The wound was so deep, she wanted to laugh. She could see the thick blood vessels and organs of her body were cut in half. Her own body was crumbling, scattering red blood. It almost looked fake.

"Kriem...hild..."

The last thing Brunhild saw was her sister's face, emotionless as she killed her.

<Brunhild...!>

The dragon beat the air with his wings. He rushed to Brunhild like a gale, taking her in his jaws before she could hit the floor. Still with the princess in his mouth, he faced Kriemhild, who had just finished swinging down her sword.

The dragon glared at Kriemhild, eyes burning with hatred.

Kriemhild raised her sword once more. It was a counterattacking stance. Bernstein judged that she was striking to kill. Just one step forward, and a blow from the holy sword would burn the dragon with its slash in passing.

But the dragon did not attack.

He prioritized saving Brunhild over his hate for Kriemhild.

Still with the princess in his jaws, he flew backward. Flapping his wings, he soared upward with a great gust of wind.

He broke through the stained glass behind him, meaning to escape from there.

Kriemhild immediately realized the dragon was trying to get away.

She plunged forward with her blade, but it was too late.

The dragon broke the prismatic glass and flew off into the night sky.

The holy sword stabbed through air, and rainbow rain sprinkled down.

No matter how she tried, her sword would not reach him now.

The dragon turned his back to Kriemhild and flew even higher and farther into the sky.

He just had to get away from the royal villa. Kriemhild would soon come after him.

With the princess in his mouth, the amber dragon flew rapidly through the sky. He escaped to the forest, far from the royal villa.

He leaned the princess against a great tree to have her rest.

<Brunhild! Hold on, Brunhild!> he called out to her, but there was no response.

This was the blunder of a lifetime. Despite being alert and aware of the attacker right in front of them, the amber dragon had been completely unable to move. Because he had the body of a dragon, he'd been afraid of the dragonslaying sword. Dragons, as creatures, were instinctively afraid of God's Power—that held true even for Bernstein, who was not a pure dragon.

Brunhild's wound was too deep—so deep, it was strange she was still faintly breathing. She could well die after one more blink.

The amber dragon felt such deep regret, he blurted out in a groan, <I can't let this happen...>

For Brunhild to be slain by her sister—

Back in the basement, he had listened as Brunhild had spoken so happily of her sister.

Brunhild trying to cure the corrosion hadn't been for her own sake, either. She had been trying to become queen herself to save her sister, since she had been able to see an ominous shadow ahead in the future where her sister became queen. That was why she'd had to cure the corrosion. Bernstein had watched as she'd shorted herself on sleep to research medicines.

For her to be killed by that sister, despite how everything had been for her and Brunhild's love for her—

The amber dragon knew no greater sorrow.

But heedless of his feelings, the pulse of Brunhild's life was getting weaker and weaker.

He wanted to grovel to God.

But in the nighttime forest, there was no God for him to cling to.

He wished he were a god himself. But Bernstein was just a dragon.

He had horns, he had wings, he had a tail, and he had fangs. That was all.

Even if he could fight, he couldn't save a life.

He wished he could at least share with the princess the unnecessarily long lifespan peculiar to dragons.

That was when something Brunhild had said came to his mind. While they had been researching in the basement, he had heard her say, <There are many mysterious effects of dragon's blood that are not yet understood.>

The dragon decided to make a gamble.

He scratched at his own throat with his long claws, and his blood spilled out. He poured it so it dripped over Brunhild's wound.

Dragon's blood was powerful vital energy. It could even grant life to one who was on the verge of death. But that was a bet with incredibly bad odds.

Dragon's blood was also a powerful poison. If 10,000 people had it spilled on them, then 9,999 would die.

The amber dragon bet on the chance that the princess would survive.

He poured his blood into her—as if he were sharing his life.

Brunhild's consciousness was in deep darkness.

It was cold, and it felt like her body was rapidly chilling.

She became frightened and ran through the darkness. But no matter how far she went, the darkness never cleared.

She finally gave up and collapsed. She thought she would just get colder and colder.

But that was when a light suddenly appeared out of nowhere.

The light of the flame warmed Brunhild's chilled body.

Feeling something warm on her eyelids, Brunhild opened her eyes.

The night had dawned and the sunlight was streaming in. What she'd felt on her eyelids was the warmth of the sun.

She wondered why she was alive. She remembered being cut down and dying.

The amber dragon was slumbering, nestled up to her. There was a scar on his neck.

She looked at her clothes. There was dried blood stuck on them. Her hair and skin were the same. From the color of it, it was clear it was not human blood.

That made Brunhild understand what had happened.

She stroked the head of the sleeping dragon.

<Thank you, my dragon...>

*　*　*

There was a pretty stream nearby, so Brunhild cleaned herself off there.

She returned to the base of the tree right as the amber dragon was opening his eyes.

<Thank your good fortune,> he said. <You won a gamble with poor odds.>

Brunhild shook her head. <I'll thank not my fortune, but you.>

<I merely poured poison into you.>

This dialogue didn't seem to have much point to Brunhild, so she approached the amber dragon and laid a kiss on his claws. That was her way of expressing the utmost respect she could.

The amber dragon said, not at all that displeased, <If you're going to kiss me, I'd rather it be on the lips.>

<Don't get carried away,> Brunhild chided the crude dragon.

The amber dragon asked, <Well then, what do we do now?>

<We can't stay in the forest forever. We have to go back to town.>

<Then what do we do?>

<I...want to know why Kriemhild tried to kill me.>

<Give it up.> The amber dragon remembered the look on Kriemhild's face when she had attacked the royal villa. He recalled her eyes had been dark and hollow. It had been uncanny. <You should avoid any more involvement with her.>

<My hunch is telling me the same. But that's precisely why I think I must do something... I always did sense something dark in her becoming queen. If something terrible is happening to her, then I must do something right away.>

<I saved your life. So long as it's clear Kriemhild is after your life, involving yourself with her is practically throwing it away again. Do you mean to put my devotion to waste?>

<Ah-ha-ha... You hit me where it hurts.> Brunhild smiled wryly. <As to that, all I can say is I'm sorry.>

The amber dragon sighed. It seemed he couldn't change Brunhild's mind when it came to her sister. <Then there's nothing to be done. I will acquiesce to your desires and accompany you as your servant.>

<You're still going to follow me? You're the one with no reason to stay...>

<Without me, you're sure to meet an untimely death.> The amber dragon spread his wings and flew into the air. <Let's go get some clothes.>

Brunhild's dress had been cut, and by transforming into a dragon, Bernstein had lost his clothing once more.

Chapter
2

Returning to the day of the coronation ceremony—

After a long embrace with her elder sister, they parted ways, and Kriemhild left the royal villa.

At noon, she arrived at the royal castle. Now the coronation ceremony for welcoming Kriemhild as the new queen would be held. The ceremony was small-scale, and only the chief vassals of the royal castle were allowed to participate. This was the way of the kingdom.

Once again, Kriemhild thought it was strange. Looking at various foreign countries, no others held such a closed coronation. Normally, the whole country would celebrate the new ruler.

For the sake of the ceremony, Kriemhild was welcomed into the throne room.

Kriemhild knelt before the empty throne. Her mother couldn't attend the ceremony, being on her sickbed—though Kriemhild had known things would be like this. She decided that once the ceremony was over, she would go to her mother. The sisters had been refused all this time, no matter how many times they had requested to see their mother, but once she was queen, nobody could stop her.

The chief vassals stood in rows to the side of the throne.

The famed twelve knights of the kingdom, and the knight captain who commanded them, Alois, were all there.

The old retainer Warren, with the crown in hand, stood beside the throne.

All wore stiff expressions.

With the atmosphere strangely dark, the coronation ceremony began.

Crown in hand, Warren came before Kriemhild.

The crown shone dully in the old retainer's hands.

Kriemhild somehow had a bad feeling about this. Even she, who did not possess the eye of god, was shivering.

Oh no, this isn't…

Kriemhild tried to back away.

But Warren was quicker, and he carried out the crowning.

He set the crown on top of her head and told her, "Congratulations on your accession to the throne."

Just then, a voice rang in her head.

It was a woman's voice ordering Kriemhild this:

Offer yourself to the kingdom.

Instantly, her body was no longer her own.

"What…?" Kriemhild asked, confused.

Warren answered, "That is the voice of the First Queen."

He began to explain in a low voice. "The First greatly feared a single individual bearing great powers, since the evil dragon that once ruled this kingdom was very much that. If someone with great power were to go out of control, the peace of the kingdom could not be maintained. And so the First made that crown."

The voice of the First Queen bound Kriemhild's body with invisible powers. This made Kriemhild remember a mysterious legend about the First Queen.

They said that the queen's charming voice had held sway over the hearts of those who heard it, and that during her golden era, her command had been like an order from God, able to bind any living creature to her word…

Kriemhild tried to take the crown off. But when she made to touch it, her hands wouldn't move.

"You will not be able to touch it or to break it, since that would be classified as an act of wrong against the future of the kingdom," said Warren. "Any acts that are not in service of the future of the kingdom are forbidden to the queen."

"You mean that the First made such an evil crown?" Kriemhild asked.

"Yes… Although later generations have improved it, expanding the interpretation of what qualifies as an act of wrong against the kingdom."

Kriemhild understood that that was the problem. This crown had most likely originally only had the role of preventing royal authority from running amok. Then it had been altered by people of later generations—from the way he spoke, by Warren—and abused.

"I understand now why our mother was unable to care for us sisters…"

She had most likely become a slave to this crown.

Kriemhild cursed her own naïveté. It seemed that wicked schemes were swirling around in this royal castle.

"Warren, please answer me. What would you have me do, putting this crown on me?"

"To serve the kingdom, just like the many queens before you. And…" Warren came to the issue at hand. "I will have you kill Princess Brunhild."

"What are you talking about…? Why would you say such a thing…?"

Warren put a hand to his mouth. "I suppose I should begin with the fact that the Miracle of Life is beginning to disappear from this country."

The Miracle of Life was the panacea that would drive away all illness. It was a medicine that had spread all over the kingdom.

"The Miracle of Life is beginning to disappear…? That couldn't be." Kriemhild argued back emphatically. "The Miracle is simple to make. Since if the queen, who has God's Power, touches water, then that turns into the Miracle. I've heard that now that I have become queen, I'll be able to turn water into the Miracle, too."

"Only the First was ever able to perform such a feat. The Second and beyond, when touching water, could not turn it into the Miracle. Even with the Power of God in their bodies, they couldn't handle it as well as the First…"

"Please don't lie to me. That would mean we haven't been able to make the Miracle ever since the death of the First over seventy years ago. It would be strange that it hadn't run out long ago. But the Miracle of Life is used widely through the kingdom, is it not?"

"That was thanks to the devotion of generations of queens."

Kriemhild shivered.

She sensed something sinister in the word *devotion*, something different from the original meaning of the word.

"That reminds me that you have been seeking to visit your predecessor for some time." Warren courteously prompted Kriemhild out of the crown room. "Let me guide you to her."

The room she was guided to was a bleak one, very different from the queen's private quarters.

There weren't even the minimal furnishings. There was a little bed in the small room, and there slept her mother.

"Mother…"

Kriemhild sensed something was strange. This room was not at all appropriate for a queen. No—it wasn't even fit to be a room for a servant. It did not feel at all lived-in.

But Kriemhild didn't care right now that those things didn't feel right. Her mother, whom she had been unable to see for so long, was before her. And she was lying there, ill. Kriemhild was so worried.

She rushed up to the bed and said to her mother, "It's been so long. I'm your daughter, Kriemhild. Mother, your health…"

Kriemhild stopped there.

Because she understood there was no longer any need to speak with her.

Her mother, before her, slept with an unnatural look.

Kriemhild's eyes moved to the blanket. It was strangely flat.

Timidly, she peeled it back.

She had made up her mind that she would cry no more.

She hated herself for being weak.

She hated herself for constantly relying on her sister's aid.

In order to become strong, she had stopped crying.

Or so she had thought.

"Ah… Ahh…"

Kriemhild sank down on the spot. Her legs were weak.

The tears came and wouldn't stop.

The fear of what was before her easily shattered Kriemhild's brave determination.

The queen had no body.

All that lay in the bed was her head.

Underneath the blanket she had peeled back, there was nothing.

As Kriemhild was wordless with terror, Warren explained, "Since the second generation, the queens have been unable to create the Miracle by touching water. Therefore, we have been turning their bodies into the Miracle."

Warren's voice traveled right past Kriemhild's head.

Even though he was right beside her as he spoke, for some reason, his voice sounded like it was coming from a great distance.

"The Miracle that's being used in the kingdom now is made from the corpses of the past queens. By making the body that bears the Power of God into powder and dissolving it in water, we were able to turn water into the Miracle..."

"Hn..." Kriemhild automatically pressed a hand over her mouth. Her visceral disgust had caused nausea. She herself had drunk the Miracle before, multiple times.

"The bodies of the queens will fundamentally not be injured, but once they become corpses, their divinity is lost and they can be carved up. If not for that, then cutting into them while alive would have been the most efficient, but..."

"Urk...!"

Kriemhild tried to swallow the vomit that was rising in her throat, but she couldn't bear it. She vomited on the floor. Not even bothered by the sight or the smell of it, Warren continued his explanation. It seemed he had anticipated this would happen. Perhaps the queens of past generations had had the same reaction as Kriemhild.

"Now we reach the subject at hand."

Even while Kriemhild moaned and vomited, the old retainer did not stop his speech.

"When a new queen ascends to the throne, we have been making the Miracle from the corpse of her predecessor. However, a problem has come up. One year ago, when your predecessor passed away...we made your mother's body into powder and dissolved it in water, but it did not become the Miracle. We believe the cause is that the queen's aptitude for the Power of God has declined with each generation."

Apparently, their mother had actually passed a year ago.

Kriemhild had sensed herself that their aptitude had declined. They did not have the same godlike powers as the First Queen. Their bodies were invincible, but they felt pain, and neither could they control people with their voices alone.

"In order to avoid needless confusion, we hid the death of the queen, and this past year, we have been continuing to test if we could somehow make the Miracle from her corpse. But even after making everything but the head into material, we were unable to make even a drop of the Miracle. Before long, the Miracle will be lost from the kingdom. Before that happens, I would like you to acquire the material for some new Miracle."

"It can't be… But where in the world would you get material for the Miracle…?"

"It's right in front of you. It's your sister, Brunhild."

It took her time to understand what her chief vassal was saying.

"That's why we will have you kill your sister, Princess Brunhild. Since we are not capable of killing the child of God, we would like you to bring her corpse to us."

"Ridiculous… How could I do such a thing?"

But when Kriemhild tried to resist, an intense pain ran through her head. It was as if the crown were tightening around it.

Unable to stand it, Kriemhild cowered.

"Now you are unable to perform any acts that would harm the kingdom's benefit."

"S…silence…" While bearing the headache, Kriemhild said, "In the first place…if you couldn't make the Miracle from Mother's corpse, then you might not be able to make it from my sister's, either."

"That may be the case. But we won't know until we test it. In order to maintain supply of the Miracle, we would have had to kill one of you sisters anyway."

"I would rather my head crack open and die than kill my sister."

The crown admonished Kriemhild particularly powerfully.

It hurt so much that she cried out, and then she lost consciousness.

After that, Kriemhild's struggles began.

Sleeping or waking, her head hurt as if there were constriction around it.

She continued to hear a voice.

Offer yourself to the kingdom.

That voice was hopelessly sweet and had a power that made her want to abandon herself to it. A number of times, Kriemhild came to her senses and caught herself with a longsword borne from the Power of God in hand and heading off to the royal villa. Every time, she struggled against the pain in her head and returned to the castle.

She very quickly became haggard and worn. An ordinary human certainly would have given in to the crown. Kriemhild was only able to resist it due to her love for her sister.

But even so, she could not avoid the mental fatigue. When she was completely exhausted and zoned out, Warren came to speak with her.

"It's not as if we're seeking to kill Princess Brunhild out of some petty malice."

Kriemhild looked at the old chief vassal with hollow eyes.

"We are aware this is an inhuman act. I'm sure that after death, we will not be invited to the Kingdom of Eternity. But there are wounds that will be healed by our inhumanity, lives that will be saved."

Warren's hand pointed out the window of the castle. Below the window, they could see the flourishing kingdom.

"We cannot allow the perfect kingdom the First created to end in our generation."

It had to be because she was mentally weakened at this point. She found herself thinking, *Yes, that's right.*

Even Kriemhild didn't want the Miracle to disappear from the kingdom. It was a medicine that eradicated all disease. She could imagine just what great damage would occur if it were gone. There were even cases in foreign countries of 40 percent of the population being lost due to infectious disease.

"I…believe you are all inhuman. But…I don't believe that act was born from ill will."

"So then…"

"Even so, I will not kill my sister. My current wish is that my life end as soon as possible."

Kriemhild held up her hand. When she did, a dagger of light

appeared in it. Upon turning thirteen, Kriemhild had become able to make a sword with the Power of God. She swung it down into her own heart.

"Ngh…"

But the knife would not reach her heart. Her hand stopped halfway.

Just as the crown prevented attacks against it, it also prevented attacks against her own body.

The crown tortured her head, punishing her for her suicide attempt. When the knife made from the Power of God left Kriemhild's hand, it melted away and vanished.

"How dare you…make such a cursed tool…," Kriemhild said resentfully.

Warren said to her, "Though it may be a cursed tool to you, to me, it is a holy relic."

Kriemhild thought that was true, since he could admonish the queen with this crown…

A few days passed after that. Or so she thought they had. Her sense of the passage of time had grown unstable.

Seeing Kriemhild become practically an invalid, Warren said, "I never thought you would be this stubborn. You have a strong heart."

She moved just her eyes to glare at him. "Warren…the healing sword you brought me was not a gift from our mother either, was it?" Warren had said the previous queen had died one year ago.

"It was a gift not from the previous queen but from myself. However, my desire that you live a long life is no lie. I would like you to live as long as possible, as the queen ruling this country."

"Don't you mean as your puppet…?"

Kriemhild thought he was a truly evil person.

He had tried to make her bear the Healing Blade, so he could use her as a puppet as long as possible. She could infer that all the queens since the Second had been puppets to Warren.

Before she knew it, Warren was gone from the room. These past few days, Kriemhild had suddenly fallen unconscious sometimes. It seemed that had happened just now, too.

Her thoughts were unclear. The never-ending pain made her struggle to think.

She lay vacantly in her bed in her room. She continued to hear the voice like a hallucination, on and on, and her head ached. Her body had long since reached its limits, and all she wished for was to be rid of the pain.

…I'm sure Mother struggled against the crown at first, too.

But in the end, she had given in.

There was no surprise there. She couldn't blame her at all—if she had been constantly beset by this torture.

…I'll just sleep.

Sleep was Kriemhild's only salvation.

While she was sleeping, she could hear no voices and feel no pain. Not for the sake of resting her body, but to escape, Kriemhild slept.

She had a dream.

Before she knew it, she was before the royal villa. She bore the sword of light in her hand.

Ahh, I'm having a dream of killing my sister again.

Kriemhild had often been beset by such nightmares lately. Her exhausted mind and body showed her such things. She couldn't avoid having dreams like this, since killing her sister would free her from her pain. At first, she had blamed herself for dreaming of killing her, but she no longer had the willpower for that.

Kriemhild headed to her sister. She killed the soldiers who got in her way.

It was just a dream anyway.

When she burned down the great hall, Brunhild came, bringing a dragon.

Brunhild put her utmost effort into trying to talk to her. But there was no point in talking.

Since it was a dream anyway.

Kriemhild heard a nasty voice in her head.

Offer yourself to the kingdom.

She was sick of it.

Finally, she was hearing the First's voice even in her dreams. She wished she could be left alone in dreams, at least.

If they wanted her sister's corpse that badly, she would give it to them—the sister in her dreams.

Obeying the voice of the crown, Kriemhild stepped forward to cut down her sister. When she obeyed the voice, for some reason, strength welled within her, and she was able to move more quickly than usual.

Her sister spurted blood as she fell. Even if it was in a dream, it was a sorrowful sight.

In the end, she wasn't able to obtain her corpse, since the dragon took her sister's body in his mouth and fled.

After letting her sister get away, Kriemhild sat down in the great hall.

She could no longer hear the voice from the crown. Neither could she feel any headache.

"Oh, it feels so good…"

She had never imagined that having no pain could be this amazing. Even though she was in a dream, she became tired and slept. Despite being on the hard floor, she was able to sleep comfortably for the first time in a long while.

Eventually, Kriemhild opened her eyes.

She didn't want to wake up—since if she awoke, she would see the ceiling of the royal castle that she so didn't want to see. Then she would again be tormented by the voice and the headache.

But she couldn't pretend to be asleep forever, so she was forced to open her eyes.

Yet it was not the castle ceiling that filled her view now.

It was the great hall, torn into pieces. There were signs of it having been burned all over the place.

Scattered corpses, corpses, corpses. They belonged to servants and soldiers.

Kriemhild's heart clenched. "It…can't be…"

She looked down at her hands. They were dirty with dried blood.

Her hands began to tremble. "Sister… No…ahh!"

So it wasn't a dream?

Like a sleepwalker, she had killed her own servants and burned up the royal villa…

…and then killed her sister?

"Hn…hnnnnnnnnnnnk!"

Kriemhild tore at her head.

She couldn't bear it. There was no way she could have killed the sister who had been so concerned about her.

Just who was it who had said she wanted to cure her sister's corrosion once she became queen?

Kriemhild's heart was already in tatters to begin with, and now the fact that she'd killed her sister was the final blow.

The orders of the crown echoed through the body that had lost its mind.

Offer yourself to the kingdom.

With some plain clothes in hand, Bernstein came to where Brunhild waited in the forest. He had gotten them for her.

"Did you steal them?"

"Basically."

She chose not to press him any further. She felt badly for whoever had had their clothes stolen, but this was an emergency.

They got changed. Bernstein now looked like a village man, while Brunhild was a village girl.

Bernstein gave the village girl Brunhild a disparaging look.

"What are you staring at me for?" she asked.

"Mm. There's something rather tempting about an aristocrat disguised as a village girl. How about it—why not become my wife now, and we'll live as village people?"

Brunhild said morosely, "If not for my sister, I could have considered that."

"That's too bad," Bernstein said with a smile.

"Bernstein—I think it's best you not make such jokes. When you one day have a woman you truly love, you'll be completely unable to speak seriously."

"I don't mean this in jest. I've been charmed by your beauty since the moment I first saw you. Most of all…"

"Most of all?"

"I don't want to see you sticking your nose into trouble. You already had an unfortunate upbringing to begin with. I want you to spend the rest of your life like anyone else, at least."

Even Brunhild had to feel something after hearing all that. She realized even him saying to become his wife was not entirely a joke.

"W-well, I accept your affections." Her heart was pounding a little, but she told it to settle down. "At any rate…I must save Kriemhild."

She thought back on her face-off with Kriemhild in the royal villa. There was that crown that had sparkled uncannily over her head.

"That crown…is not good at all."

Brunhild's eyes could see the future, though only dimly. But that was no more than a bonus on top of their fundamental ability. Her eyes could see the true nature of things. When she penetrated something with her vision, she could make abstract estimations about the future it would bring.

And to these eyes of hers, the crown had looked terribly evil. It had been as if a black darkness were clinging to it.

"I want to look into that crown," said Brunhild. "There must be a secret to it. I think the reason Kriemhild became like that is due to the crown."

"Research? So then should we go to the Academy?"

"No. I doubt the answer will be in the documents of the Academy, since that crown has been handed down for generations in the Siegfried family. I figure the answer will only be in the royal castle. I believe threatening a chief vassal, a close associate of the queen, will be the fastest and most certain."

"You can't propose such a difficult matter so casually. How will we approach that vassal? Will we sneak into the castle and kidnap them? I don't believe that's impossible, but the risks are too high. We don't even know if we could safely escape…"

"There's no need for us to sneak into the castle. We'll have the vassals come out for us."

"How?"

Brunhild smiled boldly. "Today is the First Queen's birthday."

Brunhild and Bernstein concealed themselves alongside a certain mountain path. It was the road the carriages would pass down when heading from the royal castle to the First Queen's anniversary party. It was also the place where the young Brunhild and Kriemhild had been attacked by assailants.

The carriages passed on by. They deliberately let a number of them pass. Brunhild got a general grasp on the rank of the people in the carriages by the coats and statures of the horses and the decorations on the carriages themselves.

When a particularly high-status carriage went by, Brunhild fired her Thunder.

The Thunder shot through the wheels of the carriage, destroying them. When the carriage came to a halt, Bernstein, as a dragon, leaned on it to tip it over. The coachman saw the dragon and fled. There were two knight guards on the carriage, and they very briefly made to fight, but the dragon was so imposing, they immediately broke and followed after the coachman.

Bernstein dragged two old men out from the carriage.

"Yeep, help…"

"Princess Brunhild…I never thought you'd still live."

Brunhild recognized those faces. They were without question senior vassals from the castle.

When the two senior vassals saw Brunhild, they shrieked quietly and apologized.

"No! It wasn't us."

"It was Warren. Warren is the one who said he would try to kill you."

While stroking the amber dragon's snout, Brunhild said, "To think they would be this frightened. It seems they will speak honestly."

The amber dragon growled at the old men. The two of them sank to the ground in fear.

After that, the two old men answered Brunhild's questions quite honestly.

She found out about the evil crown, about how the regent called Warren had controlled the queens through the generations, how Kriemhild had also fallen into his hands, and also about what made up the Miracle of Life.

"…" Brunhild was speechless.

She realized now that this kingdom held a darkness far deeper than she had imagined—and that it was about to swallow Kriemhild whole.

As Brunhild was overcome with shock, in her place, the amber dragon said to the old men, <What cruel men!>

He said imperiously, <No matter what just cause one might tout,

what you are doing is an act of blind obsession. If you ask me, having lived in the old times, illness and injury were only natural back then. Even if it is for the sake of the kingdom, that's no reason for Brunhild's family line to be sacrificed.>

The old men couldn't hear the voice of the dragon, however. All they could do was tremble before the dragon's zeal.

But Brunhild did hear it. <Thank you, Bernstein. That's enough.>

<No, not yet. I believe we should kill these men. They are carrying out acts which they should not as human beings. There's no value in such filth living.>

<I do share some of your feelings. But killing them won't change anything. Let them go, for me.>

But still the amber dragon was not convinced. He even glared at Brunhild.

Since it seemed like she would absolutely not back down, he gave in.

After letting the two old men go, the amber dragon said to Brunhild, <You're very kind.>

<I'm not kind.>

<You showed mercy to those pieces of trash. Isn't that kindness?>

Brunhild pulled out a knife and a little bottle filled with golden liquid from her pocket. The little bottle was some Miracle of Life she had procured in the village.

<I planned to torture them if they didn't answer our questions. I would hurt them with the knife and heal it with the Miracle. I was going to do that over and over. Would you still call me kind?>

The amber dragon shivered. It seemed she would do whatever it took for her sister's sake.

<I'm glad I didn't have to see you torture anyone. It might have cooled my long-held feelings.>

<Most certainly,> Brunhild said, and she put away the little bottle and the knife. <Now it's clear what we must do.>

The crown was on Brunhild's mind. <We'll destroy Kriemhild's crown. Let's free my sister from her curse.>

Brunhild rode astride the amber dragon's back.

They were headed for the party venue.

They had learned many things from hearing the two old men talk. They had more useful information than simply that about the Miracle and the crown.

It seemed that Brunhild was thought to have died.

They'd said that since Kriemhild had killed her, the knights had spent the past few days searching for her corpse.

This was their chance to launch a surprise attack.

Tonight a party would be held, inviting all the various influential aristocrats within the kingdom. The large private residence the old royal family had owned was the venue, and Queen Kriemhild would also be in attendance. Surprisingly, the queen's guard was just a few knights, and aside from the knights, it was just the old retainer Warren attending her, they'd said. Once everyone returned to the royal castle, it would be difficult to attack. Now, when their defenses were thin, was the best chance.

However, they would have to hurry to carry out this surprise attack. If they wasted time, then the senior vassals they had let get away would report about having been attacked by Brunhild.

Brunhild was certain she and the amber dragon would be able to carry out this surprise attack.

Of course, it went without saying that the dragon was strong. Brunhild lacked endurance, but since she could use Thunder, she was far stronger than an ordinary soldier. It would be child's play to send the guards at the party venue running. Brunhild felt luck was on their side.

The dragon arrived at the private residence, Brunhild on his back, right as the party was beginning.

They looked into the party venue from a window.

Brunhild could see Kriemhild, the crown atop her head.

" …"

She seemed to be dazed and stupefied. She was emotionally exhausted, believing that she had killed Brunhild. Now she was entirely a doll that would do whatever the crown—no, Warren—told her.

Seeing her sister in such a pitiful state, Brunhild felt a pang in her heart.

She wanted to save Kriemhild as quickly as possible.

<Go, Amber Dragon!>

At that order from Brunhild, the dragon replied with an easygoing <Aye.>

The dragon dramatically broke through the window glass and charged into the party venue.

The aristocrats shrieked out and ran about frantically trying to escape.

"A dragon!"

"Why is there a *dragon*?!"

"Princess Brunhild is on a dragon!"

"Why?!"

In an instant, the pleasant party turned into a scene of chaos.

Hearing the commotion, the knights came. But there really weren't many guards at the party. Most likely, it had been decided that so many imposing guards would be unbefitting for such a splendid event.

A few of the knights boldly stood up against the dragon. But the amber dragon easily routed them. Brunhild also came down from the dragon and fought with her Thunder.

Even with this much confusion going on, Kriemhild didn't even look toward the uproar. She was sitting on her chair with a hollow expression.

At this point, she had been so badly damaged that she couldn't react to any stimulation around her at all.

"Kriemhild!"

Even her sister's cry didn't reach her deeply wounded heart.

But...

"Kriemhild!"

In Kriemhild's field of view appeared her sister, racing toward her.

"Sis...ter...?" The light slowly returned to Kriemhild's eyes.

"Sister...!" Kriemhild stood up.

"Oh, Sister! I'm so glad you're alive...!" She tried to run up to Brunhild.

But she froze halfway. Pain ran through her head like a flash of light.

"Ngh..."

Offer yourself to the kingdom.

The voice made her body try to kill her sister, of its own accord—since the crown had recognized that her sister was alive.

She somehow controlled her right hand as it attempted to make the sword of Thunder.

It was an incredible act of will. It came out of her fervent desire to not hurt her sister any further.

Kriemhild fell to her knees on the spot, hugging herself to restrain herself as she cried, "Don't come near, Sister! I'll hurt you again…"

"It's all right. I'll break the crown for you now," Brunhild said gently to put her sister at ease.

Brunhild's victory was assured.

That was right as the amber dragon was incapacitating the final knight in the venue.

The only hostile force to remain was Warren, who was at Kriemhild's side.

Warren stood before Kriemhild. It seemed he was trying to obstruct Brunhild and the dragon.

But what could a mere elderly retainer do?

The dragon approached and breathed his flames at Warren. He meant to threaten him and drive him away.

But…

Warren's long coat fluttered, and he walked into the flames. The coat must have been made from special material, as there was no sign of it catching flames. In fact, the coat was even putting them out.

The amber dragon howled, <Old man, I will commend only your bravery in not cowering before me.>

He tried to snap at Warren as he approached. He meant not to kill him, but to drive him away with enough wounds to prevent him acting.

Seeing the great jaws coming toward him, Warren muttered softly, "How slow."

The amber dragon's vision shook wildly.

He understood belatedly—a powerful knee strike had hit him from below his jaw.

Warren had kicked him. A strike that seemed impossible from such an old frame had closed the dragon's great maw.

<!>

The completely unexpected counterattack left the dragon in a momentary confusion. And even without that, his brain had been rattled with a shock like a hammer strike. Warren did not overlook that opportunity.

"Two, then."

Warren pulled out from underneath the coat he wore two swords that shone with faint light. They were stilettos that had been modified for throwing. There was a *whoosh* as the blades whipped through the air to pierce the dragon's jaw from below. They kept the dragon from opening his mouth.

"These blades were processed with the Power of God and will weaken a dragon. I could have killed the child of God with them, too."

With two of them, he could seal the dragon's jaws shut.

<You foul...>

Even if he couldn't use his jaws, the dragon still had claws that were sharper than blades. He had the strike of his tail, which could break bones. The amber dragon unerringly used those weapons. He was no longer considering restraint. He understood that with this opponent, it was kill or be killed.

But his understanding came too late. No—he couldn't even be sure if he could have won if he'd known that from the beginning.

Warren avoided all the dragon's attacks by a hair.

It was as if he could see the future. But that was not in fact the case.

He could tell what sorts of attacks would come based off the faintest signs shown by the dragon's musculature. Each time he dodged, a stiletto pierced the dragon's flesh. In the blink of an eye, the amber dragon became a pincushion and fell. The blades that housed a faint amount of God's Power stole away the dragon's strength.

Warren was no old minister—he was an old soldier.

Once, there had been countless dragons lurking in the kingdom, and they had been wiped out by the First Queen. That was mostly true, but it was not well known that in actuality, there had been a small elite squad who had assisted the queen in this duty. For the dragons that hadn't required the queen's efforts, that squad had cleaned them up.

Warren had been a member of that squad ever since he'd been a boy. And despite being a boy, he had been a dragonslayer second only to the First Queen.

With age, the strength of his youth had left him. But he was still no inferior to a mere fifteen-foot-tall dragon.

A few seconds since the battle had begun, and the dragon fell. After falling, the amber dragon realized—this man was most certainly the boy dragonslayer who had once tried to kill him.

"…"

Brunhild was the one who was speechless—so much that she thought she was having a bad dream.

Though belatedly, now Brunhild's eyes saw something nasty in this chief vassal. The old man had cleverly hidden his own strength.

The soldier looked at her. Their eyes locked. Brunhild's eyes read a certain future.

That was the future of her loss.

"Urk…"

But even so, Brunhild wove the lightning in her fingers and threw it. With the seasoned warrior glaring at her, she was still able to put up slight resistance despite being overwhelmed thanks to her wholehearted desire to save her sister.

"Wagh!"

But Brunhild was an amateur at combat. Archery was a royal art, so she had fired a bow before, but such technique was largely useless in combat.

The old soldier casually avoided the Thunder. And then he stepped up before Brunhild and pierced her vitals with a stiletto. The intense pain knocked Brunhild right out.

"Sister! Ahh, it can't be!"

Seeing Brunhild faint, Kriemhild broke down.

While watching with cold eyes, Warren sorted out the situation.

This was the perfect chance.

If he could control Kriemhild now and have her kill Brunhild, it would be complete.

But despite that—

—Warren could not do that.

Unfortunately, there were the eyes of the aristocrats. There had been a party going on here just moments ago.

He couldn't have the queen kill someone in front of the aristocrats.

So then should he take Brunhild somewhere deserted and kill her?

He couldn't. The girl had made too much of a dramatic entrance. After gathering the attention of the aristocrats, he couldn't carry her off someplace deserted…

He doubted Brunhild had considered before her attack what would occur if she lost, but ultimately, her bold surprise attack was about to save her life.

He was frustrated at being unable to make his move when the results he sought were right in front of him.

Irritated, Warren gave instructions to the knights. "Escort the dragon and princess to the royal castle. Their execution will be determined after the necessary procedures."

That was the most Warren could do.

It was just frustrating. He told himself it was nothing to worry about.

Even just having captured Brunhild put the situation extremely in his favor.

There was no need to rush to kill her.

After confining them in the castle, he should just quietly kill her along with her dragon.

After giving that order to the knights, he was struck with intense numbness.

I very much do not want to get any older, he thought.

Chapter

3

The current royal family in the kingdom was a clan by the name of the Siegfrieds. They were the lineage with the Dragonslaying Queen as their ancestor.

However, before the Siegfried family, there had been a different royal family.

That royal family was now in ruin. This was due to their bad name: The most inept ruler, called the Dragon King, had been born from that royal family. About one hundred years ago, he had massacred many people. Ever since then, that family had come to be persecuted as the clan of the foolish king. The Dragon King had killed so many because his body had been under the control of an evil dragon, but that was not at all taken into consideration.

This low-ranking knight who called himself Anima was in fact one of that clan. He was seventeen years old.

Anima was not his real name. If he were to reveal his real name, then he wouldn't be able to stay in this country. Unfortunately, he had been given the same name as the foolish king. His parents, who believed in the innocence of the foolish king, had given him that name. Anima saw it as a real nuisance. The parents who had named him were no longer in this world. They had lost their lives due to persecution. It was outrageous, when they hadn't even been such close relations to the king.

Anima had wound up all alone, with no living relatives.

The only thing he owned was a single spear.

Anima hated the Siegfried family. The fake royal family, called the Siegfrieds, believed they had banished them, the *true* royal family. That was what he had been taught, that that teaching was true, in one view.

He resented them. His clan had suffered because of the Siegfried family.

But he didn't think to do anything about it. Having been persecuted all his life, Anima had his hands full just getting by. Concealing his name, his birth, and his past, he had somehow managed to attain the rank of knight. He figured he would cling to that until he died. Revenge wouldn't fill his stomach.

That day, Anima was on guard at the dungeon cells at the royal castle.

As he was casually fulfilling his duty, a girl was brought into the dungeon.

It was a girl with white hair and red eyes.

The ones to escort her in were high-ranking knights.

Anima asked, "Is this girl a criminal or something?"

"She's someone Her Majesty Kriemhild will be personally executing later. Is any further explanation necessary for a low-ranked knight?"

Anima bowed his head. "No, sir. It's as you say."

He had no urge to pry further. He would choose toeing the line over actual struggle.

The girl was restrained, then thrown into a cell that was adjoining the guardroom.

Anima watched the girl as she had her hands tied behind her back and was put into the cell.

It bothered him.

She hasn't been eating much.

The girl's face was pallid, her body small, her bones apparent. She looked to him as if she were starving.

Starvation largely did not exist in the kingdom these days.

The Miracle of Life, created by the queen, did away with all wounds and sickness. It could even cure starvation. Since it had spread so widely among the people, people fundamentally couldn't starve anymore.

That was, so long as you were not persecuted and deliberately made unable to acquire the Miracle.

Anima knew the pain of starvation. And he figured if she was starving, then most likely, the girl's station was low, just as his had once been.

And they had said that this pitiable girl would be executed by the hand of the new queen of the Siegfried family.

It kind of felt as though he was the one who was going to be killed.

…I have a grudge against the Siegfried family.

So it was Anima's own sort of revenge.

Once it was night, Anima freed the thin girl from her cell, avoiding the eyes of the other guards.

There were various reasons Anima was able to do this. He was certain that even if he let this girl go, he would not be blamed for it. The knight who was his superior was partial to him. Since Anima just wanted to live a peaceful life, his behavior was particularly good. He had never once defied his superiors. The decisive reason was that one of the knights who was on duty at the dungeon that night was a man with extremely bad behavior. If Anima let the girl go, that man would certainly be the one first suspected. If not for that, the timid Anima would never have done something so bold as to let this girl escape.

He brought the girl outside the guardroom and handed her the sword that had been confiscated from her.

"Get out of here."

But the girl didn't move.

She said to Anima, "You're a knight, aren't you…?"

"So what?"

"If you're a knight, then your job is to escort me. Don't toss me out and then go."

The arrogance of this remark left Anima dumbfounded.

"D-don't be ridiculous!" Of course he was angry. He'd thought she might thank him for letting her go. Who would imagine she would demand more of him, of all things? "Just who do you think you are?"

"Ha-ha, a princess, perhaps."

She said something so ridiculous so boldly, Anima was stunned. At the same time, he also found himself thinking that she wasn't lying. An ordinary person would be too embarrassed to say she was a princess.

But if she was a princess, then it made sense that she was about to be executed by the queen's hand. Sometimes, the kingdom would be attacked by foreign nations. These invasions targeted the unique technologies the kingdom possessed, as well as the Miracle of Life. The queen, who controlled the Power of God, had repelled everything to resolve all large-scale conflict, but small-scale conflict was ongoing in various areas. It could be this was a foreign princess who had been captured.

It was only natural that Anima would assume this princess was not his own nation's princess.

Precisely because he had once been of the royal line, he knew the Siegfried family all had black hair and black eyes.

The girl before him had white hair and red eyes.

Well, whoever this girl was, he had no intention of getting himself any deeper in this. He'd just let the girl go as revenge against the Siegfried family.

"Be grateful that I just let you go," he said, then left the girl in the town at night and made to return to the dungeon.

From behind him, he heard the sound of a wet cough.

When he turned around, the girl was covering her mouth with her hand. She was coughing up blood.

She fell to her knees on the ground. It seemed she had some kind of illness. He could tell she wasn't strong enough to stand.

"H-hey. Are you okay?" Anima panicked and ran up to the girl.

He had no way of knowing, but the healing sword leaving her hands was the cause of her health deteriorating.

Ah...what am I doing?

Now that he had turned around and run up to her, he could no longer abandon her. He had to take this girl back home and at least give her some of the Miracle...

Anima quickly finished up his work and took the girl back to his house, where he had her drink the Miracle. The girl resisted weakly, saying she would not drink it, but he forced her to take it. Her life might be in danger, so he had to do whatever it took. But for some reason, the Miracle that was supposed to heal all illnesses didn't work. Regarding this, the girl explained only that "it's due to my constitution."

So Anima had the girl drink a medicine that he had compounded himself. He had some knowledge of medicine. Mysteriously, it seemed this worked a little. The girl's condition improved, and she was able to fall asleep.

While watching the girl's face as she slept holding her sword, Anima muttered, "I never wanted to get involved with some princess, though."

The foolish king who had caused the downfall of their clan had died protecting a lady, after all.

Anima's dream was to achieve a normal sort of happiness. He would become a normal knight, earn a normal living, marry a normal wife, have normal children, age normally, and die normally.

Having a princess here seemed like it was enough to destroy his dream, all on its own.

But he couldn't abandon her. Seeing how thin the arms that stuck out from underneath the blanket were, he just couldn't do it. Her arms were not healthy ones. They were arms that hadn't been seen in this kingdom for a long time—his own arms, long ago.

He wound up wondering just what kind of horrible fate she had met in this kingdom.

"...Damn it!"

After tucking those thin arms under the blanket, Anima decided to sleep on the floor.

The next morning, even after Anima awoke, the princess was still asleep.

So he began to make a breakfast for two.

Around the time breakfast was done, the princess opened her eyes. "Thank you for yesterday. I was belated in thanking you, despite how you freed me from that prison."

"You couldn't thank me then, could you?" She had been coughing up blood. He understood that much.

Anima set out the breakfast on a wooden desk. "Well, eat. I made some stuff that's good for your health."

Looking down at the breakfast, the girl got a strained smile. "Th... thank you..."

Everything on the breakfast table was foods she didn't like. It was a plain meal, mostly beans and vegetables. Only the token dried meat seemed appealing to her.

"I appreciate the sentiment, I suppose… I'm not very hungry."

When the princess tried to reject the meal, Anima said quietly, "If you don't eat, you'll die."

There was darkness in his words.

He was intimidating in a way only one who had experienced the pain of starvation could be, overwhelming the princess.

"Someone with malnutrition like you has to eat whatever they can. I don't care if you're a princess or what—you can't be picky."

"Nutrients, hmm…? You say the same thing as my servant."

That must have reminded her of something.

The princess picked up the wooden spoon and fork and began eating. While she had tears in her eyes and spent a long time at it, she did properly finish the meal.

That was all it was, but Anima saw her in a slightly more positive light.

After spending quite some time to finish the meal, the girl said, "I truly am sorry for making you even cook for me. Thanks to you, my condition has improved. I think I can leave now."

"Don't lie. It's completely obvious that you're still quite ill."

Even just her complexion was very pallid. While she had accepted the healing sword from Anima, it had yet to fully take effect. It would immediately lose effect if she let go of it, and she would need a few days to receive its benefits once again.

"But there are people waiting for me. I must go save them."

"Where are they?"

"At the castle. Two of them."

"Give up on it." If it had been something minor, he had felt that as a knight, he would resolve it for her—but it seemed she was involved in a greater incident than he'd imagined. "If they're imprisoned at the castle, then there's no saving them now."

"I can't give up on them."

"Is that right? Then do what you want. But I won't let you leave right away."

"Why not?"

"Since if you go outside, you'll just wind up collapsing right away."

He understood that letting this princess stay for a long time would heighten the risk of getting dragged into trouble. But even so, he said, "You can stay here a little longer. If you push yourself and go out and die…then it would make my saving you pointless."

The girl's condition had improved, but that was just compared with the day before. If she walked around outside, she would immediately use up all her strength.

She understood that, too. If she were being honest, she had already gotten some sense that even if she left right now, she wouldn't be able to save her friends.

So she was glad of Anima's offer. And it wasn't only because of her poor health. She was being pursued, so it was very helpful to be able to stay at Anima's house as a refuge.

"I won't stay too long." Gazing at her sword, the girl said, "I will leave here in three days. After that, I should be able to move on my own."

"All right."

"So you'll take care of me for three days. May I ask your name?"

"Anima."

Hearing that, the princess thought it odd.

She knew that Anima meant *nameless* in the old language.

The princess waited, assuming he would ask her name in return, but he never did.

Anima's rule was that he would not do to others what unpleasant things had been done to him.

So began their three days living together.

Anima was used to seeing to the ill. And the princess did as he asked. It seemed she had decided to be obedient, so as to recover as quickly as possible—though she would give him bitter looks during mealtimes only.

But still, the princess would do as he said and would make sure to eat the things she hated.

At night, when going to sleep, the princess in bed would say to Anima on the floor, "I truly am sorry I can't do anything…but I would be glad if you did not expect me to sleep with you."

"Why would I expect that from a sick girl? Just go to bed."

Anima was a boy around that age. He had as much desire as anyone else, and spending the night with a woman would get him excited. If it had been an ordinary woman sleeping over at his house, he certainly wouldn't have been able to stand it.

But he wasn't so deviant as to lust after a sick person.

Anima thought that if he could, he would like to have the princess attended to by an actual doctor. But there were no doctors in this country. So he decided he would at least just have her properly eat her meals.

Because of his past, Anima paid much more attention than others to healthy eating. The princess's health slowly improving may have been thanks to the healthy meals based on his experiential knowledge.

The second day came.

On that day, the princess's health was not so bad.

As she was slowly walking around the house in attempt to regain her strength, she found the cellar.

There was no deep meaning in her peeking into it.

There were countless books on medicine inside. Books were normally so expensive, a commoner would never have multiple. But medical books were the one exception. With the appearance of the Miracle of Life, any type of medical book had wound up just about worthless. Anima was now of a station where he could acquire the Miracle of Life, but the terror of the disease he had caught when young had traumatized him. He had studied medicine himself in preparation for the time when he would once again be persecuted and become unable to acquire the Miracle of Life.

As she was moving around the books, the princess found it.

It was a single dusty spear.

"…" The princess was dumbfounded, gazing at the spear.

She was probably like that a long time.

So when Anima came over to her, she didn't even notice. "So this is where you were."

"…What's this spear?"

"It's just a spear."

"No." Being of the royal family, the girl knew what this spear really was. "This is not simply a spear. It's a magic spear, with the power of the spirits. The former bearer of this spear was the best knight in the realm."

"So you have an eye for these things, Princess."

The princess realized who Anima really was.

"Why do you not use this spear? You're leaving it covered in dust? This spear will give you strength. So long as you have it, you don't have to remain a mere low-ranked knight. Even becoming the knight captain would be no dream."

"The owner of that spear was killed," Anima said dispassionately. "That was because he had strength. He died dramatically, in a manner befitting a hero."

He continued, spitting it out. "It's a stupid way to die. He talked big about how he would protect the royal family, but in the end, he couldn't protect anyone. And if you're talking about stupidity, my family is just as stupid. They've been passing this thing on for generations. The idiots believed this spear was sure to protect them. And it never did—they all died except for me."

The princess quietly listened to Anima's curses.

"I don't want to become some fabled hero," he said. "I don't aspire to that. I inherited this spear from my father, but I have no attachment to it. I just keep it to sell if I ever really need to eat."

At this point, Anima realized his voice had become dark and low. His hatred for his relatives and the spear had unconsciously made his words heavier. So he said his next remark lightly, purely as a joke.

"If you're a princess, then I actually was a prince."

The princess was unable to reply. She didn't even laugh scornfully at his joke. Anima took her silence to mean that it wasn't funny.

"But I don't care about the nation or the people. My dream is just to be happy in a normal way. As a normal knight, I'll make a normal living, marry a normal wife, have normal children, get old normally, and die normally. I don't need a magic spear for that dream."

The princess did not laugh at the old prince's normal dream.

"…Then you should let this spear be forgotten with time."

The third day came.

Anima's care bore fruit, and the girl had regained a fair amount of energy.

"I'll accompany you on your errands, as exercise."

Had she said that on a whim, or was it something else?

They headed out shopping together. He did tentatively have the princess carry the basket, but she had been weak to begin with, so she wasn't able to carry that much. Seeing her walk around with just two or three fruits in a basket that could carry a whole load of vegetables made him suspect maybe she was doing it as a joke.

When they came back from shopping, whatever the princess was thinking, she stood with him in the kitchen and tried to help him with cooking. With a kitchen knife in hand, she tried to peel the skin off a vegetable. He was quite nervous about her handling of the knife, however, so he immediately took it away from her.

"Just wait quietly. It's creepy when you try to help," Anima said, but he was privately glad.

Part of his dream was to "marry a normal woman." It wasn't as if he was looking at this girl in that way, but he did think, if he had a wife, maybe it would be like this… Although considering how incompetent this princess was, maybe his dream of having children was closer to coming true than his dream of having a wife.

Just a little, just a very little bit, he was starting to enjoy himself.

However, the princess doing such things was not out of a brand-new desire to be kind. In her own way, she felt guilty toward the old royal family. Anima shouldn't actually have been living this way.

Three days had passed by. The princess had regained quite a bit of her energy.

"Thank you very much for these past three days."

She was trying to leave Anima's house. It seemed she had no strong feelings about that. In fact, it seemed like she was trying to leave as soon as possible… Anima felt a prickle in his heart.

It had only been three days of taking care of her. But the time had given him a modest piece of mind. The truth was, he'd already felt that the very first night the princess had come.

It wasn't that she had done anything for him—but just her being there had made him feel at ease. Having abandoned his birth, his past, and his name, living without a single relative, it had been the first time he'd felt reassured.

As she was about to leave, Anima said to the princess, "If you're ever in trouble…you can come again."

He knew he was offering her too much support when they had only known each other for three days.

But they had been together for three days. Maybe she wasn't a friend, but she was no longer a stranger.

The princess did not say she would come again.

"I won't come to this house again."

"I...I see. But if we ever meet again—"

"...That reminds me, I forgot to tell you my name."

"At this point, you don't have to..."

"Listen, my name is Brunhild."

Time stopped for him.

Brunhild.

That was the name Anima most did not want to be involved with—

—since the downfall of his clan had begun with involvement with a woman named Brunhild.

Brunhild knew that, too.

That was why her self-introduction was her farewell.

"I don't think I want to see a lowborn scum like yourself ever again," she spat coldly, and then she left.

Once Brunhild was out of sight, anger slowly began to well up in him. "Talking like that to me..."

He didn't appreciate the last thing she had said to him—

—that she never wanted to see him again.

Anima understood—

—she hadn't wanted to destroy his dream of living a normal life.

"Lowborn scum...? She's such a terrible liar..."

But he had no choice but to accept the offer made to him—because his dream was to have a normal life.

Anima decided to forget about Brunhild and live on as a humble knight.

Chapter

4

The boy stood alone in a sea of blood.

Collapsed buildings. Scattered wreckage. Cracked streets.

Countless bodies were lying there. They were all those who had been his friends and acquaintances.

Until its destruction, this had been a little village.

It had been attacked by a dragon.

He had learned afterward that upon the death of the evil dragon that had ruled the kingdom, some of the dragon's private army, which had been stationed all over the country, had apparently begun acting on their own.

Although this dragon was already dead—it was the very thing that lay collapsed in the center of the village, bleeding from its neck. The blood that filled the village was mostly from that dragon. It was over fifty yards long.

The boy had killed it.

He didn't know why or how he had been able to do it. When he'd seen it, he'd thought he could win. He had picked up a knife unconsciously, and before he knew it, he had been killing the dragon. Perhaps the boy was a genius.

A dragonslaying genius.

If that was what he was, then it seemed a genius wasn't as big a deal as he'd thought—if he had only been able to kill the dragon and he hadn't even been able to protect the village.

That evening, the royal knights came.

Leading them was a woman in her late twenties. She had a vassal with bad legs serving her.

Seeing the disastrous scene of the village, the woman said, "Did you kill the dragon?"

"Yeah. It wasn't that big a deal."

That wasn't a bluff. It really hadn't been a big deal.

The woman went to her knees before the boy. She didn't even care about the blood all over the ground dirtying her knees, even though she was probably an aristocrat.

The woman drew the boy close and embraced him.

And then she said, "I'm sorry we were too late in coming. You must have been scared."

He wondered what she was talking about.

Even while fighting a dragon over ten times bigger than him, the boy had felt no fear.

The woman took the boy in. She was gathering orphans and even taking care of them.

That woman was the Dragonslaying Queen.

After being taken in by the queen, the boy was assigned to the dragonslaying support squad. He had requested it himself. He thought that was probably where he belonged. At the very least, he was more cut out for it than doing farmwork in an orphanage.

There were many people in the support squad who admired the queen. They all said the same thing.

"She's a genius."

"There's no one her better when it comes to killing dragons."

A genius? Then she was no big deal, either.

He heard the queen say this:

"I want to make everyone in the kingdom happy."

A mere genius couldn't make that dream come true—just as he hadn't been able to protect his village.

But—

Eventually, the boy learned.

There were people in the world who were beyond genius.

What should they be called? The boy could only think of one word.

God.

The boy saw the queen in her golden age.

She lightly waved her right hand. The light it emitted eradicated a foreign army.

She touched water with her right hand. The water she touched turned to a universal panacea.

The strange ring of her voice would cause all who heard it to feel happy, subordinating them to her.

Even with that much power, the queen never became a tyrant.

She only ever used that power for the sake of the kingdom's happiness.

At the time when that boy became a man, the kingdom was complete: a country with no illness or injury, never exposed to threats by foreign nations and never fearing the terror of dragons.

Looking out over the kingdom from the royal castle, the man muttered, "This has to be the Kingdom of Eternity."

The greatest paradise that humanity could create unfurled beneath his eyes.

Tears spilled from his eyes. For the first time since he had been born, a scene of beauty had made him cry.

He had to preserve this perfect beauty. He felt that was his mission, as someone born in this kingdom.

But soon after having created her utopia, the queen died. That was due to the corrosion of the Power of God.

At the very end, even God did not last long.

That was when the old soldier woke up.

Warren had returned from the party venue to the royal castle.

He recalled he had tried to take a bit of a rest in his room...but it seemed that, unaware, he had fallen into a doze. Unfortunately, getting older meant facing more physical limitations. He had worn himself out just from fighting a single dragon. More so than the physical exertion, the extreme concentration peculiar to combat had drained his energy—so much so that once the fight had been over, he hadn't been able to move.

Oh, that was right. He had to go kill that dragon.

He had ordered the knights to take the dragon and princess to the castle. He had separated them, imprisoning the dragon in the tower and the princess in the dungeon.

He hadn't had the knights kill the dragon because they didn't know how it was done. There was a trick to killing a dragon. With their powerful vitality, if you didn't hit it in the right spot, there was the risk it would rampage around with unexpected strength and be able to escape. Warren was the only one who could kill it quickly.

There was hardly anyone in the kingdom now who knew how to kill a dragon. The Dragonslaying Queen had died, and the queen's support squad had also all died, aside from Warren. Those who hadn't died in battle had died of old age. In the squad, Warren had been the youngest.

At the same time, he was also the last retainer who knew about the era of the First Queen.

Warren headed for the tower where the amber dragon was locked up.

The amber dragon was imprisoned in a room on the highest floor of the tower.

His body had been pierced with stilettos to weaken him. Being unable to exert himself, he couldn't escape.

He could hear footsteps coming up the stairs. Someone was approaching the top of the tower.

He knew quite well who had come. Most certainly, either the old soldier called Warren or a knight had come to kill him.

This was the kingdom of dragonslayers. Evil dragons could only be killed.

At the end, the amber dragon struggled. He kept trying to get the stilettos stuck into his body out. But something like this couldn't be worked out with effort or willpower.

The door opened, and someone came in.

The amber dragon was prepared for death, but…

<Ahh…how horrible…>

…the one to come in was neither the old soldier nor a knight.

It was the reigning queen, Kriemhild.

Kriemhild was also of the Siegfried clan, so she could speak the Dragon's Tongue.

Kriemhild rushed up to him and started pulling the stilettos out from his body. She only had the strength of a girl, so it took her time to get a single stiletto out.

<I'm sure this will hurt, but please bear with it.>

It was true that pulling a sword out from his body hurt. But the pain Kriemhild felt was clearly greater than the pain the amber dragon felt.

<Hn—nnnnnnngh!>

The cursed crown was torturing her. Right now, she fundamentally could not do wrong against the kingdom. As she struggled to pull out the blade, a greasy sweat oozed out of her forehead. Blood was dripping from her scalp. It seemed the blood vessels there had popped. She was bearing with the pain as she tried to let the amber dragon escape.

The dragon didn't tell her to stop—since he had to do whatever it took to escape from this tower and save Brunhild. Instead, he asked, <Why would you go this far to save me?>

<I have a request. Please take my sister and escape the kingdom. I don't know how she did it, but my sister has escaped the dungeon. Find her and flee the kingdom.>

Even as Kriemhild was moaning in pain, she pulled out the stiletto that was pinning his wings. <Please fly my sister away on your wings. There is no place for her here in this kingdom.>

That was when he once again heard footsteps coming up the stairs. This time, they were clearly those of a man. From the quality of the sound, there was no doubting they were those of a soldier.

Warren had come.

Kriemhild hurried even more to take the stilettos out. Having fewer of them piercing his body had enabled the amber dragon to struggle a little, so he helped her to get them out.

As they set about removing the final stiletto, the footsteps broke into a run. He must have noticed someone was in the tower. The amber dragon would have liked to destroy Kriemhild's crown before escaping, if possible, but he didn't have the time.

Right as they got the final stiletto out, Warren came into the room.

The amber dragon was right about to break the window and get outside, but Warren had already drawn a new stiletto. He was faster than the escaping dragon.

He threw the stiletto.

"Stop it!"

The queen's voice rang out through the tower.

Kriemhild cut between them, arms spread.

That wasn't enough to stop Warren from doing anything. He could push her away to throw a stiletto, or if he changed the angle of his throw a little, he wouldn't even need to bother shoving her aside. Kriemhild's presence, her attempt to protect the dragon, was pointless.

But despite that...

There was the sound of wingbeats. The dragon had successfully escaped.

Warren couldn't move. He stood by and watched as the dragon broke through the window.

The dragon, seen through the window, grew smaller and smaller.

Only the queen and her old retainer remained in the tower room.

Kriemhild, the black-haired queen, gazed at Warren curiously. Then she asked him, "Why...didn't you throw the sword?" She understood her own powerlessness—she couldn't even be a shield for the dragon.

Warren didn't reply, tucking the stiletto under his coat.

Kriemhild's voice as she had guarded the dragon was ringing out in Warren's head.

The boy had also once admired a black-haired queen.

The sight of her sacrificing herself to protect another had, for just a second...looked like her.

"It's a dragon! There's a dragon out!"

As Brunhild was walking in the town, she heard people yelling.

When she looked up, it was right as the amber dragon was flying through the sky over town. The amber dragon was deliberately exposing himself, flying around in order to find Brunhild.

Brunhild called the dragon's name in the Dragon's Tongue.

<Bernstein!>

Reacting to her voice, the amber dragon looked down into the town. There were a number of village girls below, but he found the white-haired one among them and dived down, taking her in his jaws.

While rising into the air, he tossed Brunhild upward.

"Wahh…"

Brunhild fell downward onto the dragon's back. The amber dragon had deftly tossed her onto a seat on his back.

In the town seen below, people were wailing. "He's kidnapped a girl!"

"Call for the knights!"

<I'm glad you're safe, Bernstein. How did you get out?>

<Your sister helped me.>

The dragon continued to fly at high speed—in a direction out of the kingdom.

<…Hey, where are we going?> Brunhild asked.

<Somewhere not in this kingdom. Anywhere is fine. You're going to live there, with me.>

<No!> Brunhild raised her voice a little. <I told you. I'm going to destroy the crown. I can't abandon my sister and run.>

<This is her wish.>

Brunhild hesitated.

<When she freed me, Kriemhild said—she wanted me to take her sister and flee the kingdom. Of course, I feel the same way.>

<But…>

<The practical issue here is that saving Kriemhild is nigh impossible, since we have no way of defeating that old soldier. I'll take you out of the country. This time, no matter how you protest, I will take you away.>

The amber dragon was thinking of when Brunhild had been captured by Warren. Being immobilized by stilettos, the dragon had only been able to watch. He didn't want to experience such powerlessness anymore, and neither did he want to let such a thing happen to Brunhild again.

<I cannot repeat that mistake…,> he muttered quietly.

Brunhild was glad to hear that. The ring of his words touched deep in her heart. <…Thank you. You truly do care for me, don't you?>

She wrapped her arms around the dragon's neck. There was clear affection and tenderness in her hands. So then the amber dragon could be at ease and flap his way out of the kingdom.

But—

<...So I'm sorry.>

The arms wrapped around his neck slid away.

The weight on his back vanished.

When he turned his head behind, thinking that it couldn't be, Brunhild had leaped from his back.

She fell upside-down toward the earth. The First Queen had been able to fly through the air without wings, but Brunhild couldn't do that.

<You fool!>

He pursued the falling Brunhild. She descended at the speed of a shooting star. He caught her in his mouth right before she hit the ground.

Still with her in his maw, the amber dragon said angrily, <You just about died.>

<I wouldn't die. My body is invincible. Well, it might hurt a little, though.>

Now that she pointed it out, it was true. It had been so sudden, he had forgotten she was physically invincible.

<But it's still an incredibly reckless thing to do!>

She spoke of it lightly...but once she had hit the ground, it would have hurt far more than just "a little."

<I had no choice. The way things were going, I was going to wind up eloping with a dragon.>

<Do you dislike me that much?>

<It's not that. I do like you. But...even so, my sister is a greater priority.>

<Do you love her?>

<Hmm. I'm not sure. When you put it like that, I don't know... but to me, protecting Kriemhild is something I take for granted, like breathing. So abandoning her isn't even an option to me.>

The amber dragon thought privately—that *was* love.

The amber dragon had lived longer than humans. He figured he had something of an understanding of love.

Even if he tried to drag Brunhild out of the country with him, she would return on her own.

The amber dragon gently lowered her, in his mouth. Her thin legs touched the ground.

<...There's no helping it. Let's put a plan together—a plan to save your sister.>

The amber dragon understood anew that they had to save Kriemhild first or he would be unable to save Brunhild.

"Brunhild!"

Anima had watched as the white-haired girl had been taken away by the amber dragon. Of course he'd assumed she was being abducted to be eaten. He couldn't hear the Dragon's Tongue.

Anima pursued the dragon and Brunhild. But it was too fast, and he was completely unable to catch up.

Running on and on, Anima finally ran out of breath and came to a stop. He hung his head, shoulders heaving. Sweat dripped down to make black marks on the ground.

"Damn it… Brunhild…," he was mumbling in frustration when someone addressed him.

"Hey, you over there."

He looked over to see a knight standing there. He was clad in armor that only high-ranked knights were allowed to wear.

That knight was one of the top twelve in the kingdom. He was of a position high enough to be aware of the kingdom's dark secrets, about the facts of the Miracle and the crown.

"You just said 'Brunhild,' didn't you?"

Anima felt his blood draining from his whole body. "Uh…I mean…"

Right now, knights all over the kingdom were searching for Brunhild.

The knight grabbed Anima's arm hard. "You're coming with me."

Anima was dragged off to the castle.

The high-ranked knight personally questioned him. Normally, a high-ranked knight would not personally be doing any questioning, but the matter of Brunhild was closely related to the kingdom's dark secrets. They would have to be someone who knew about the Miracle and such, or he wouldn't be able to conduct an interrogation.

When asked about Brunhild, Anima confessed everything honestly. It was partially self-preservation, but he also understood that even if he told them, it wouldn't help them catch Brunhild. He had just sheltered her for three days.

The high-ranked knight also seemed to figure he couldn't get much information from Anima.

"I have no more to ask you," he said, and then left the interrogation room. Anima thought it was looking like he would soon be freed.

Ten minutes after the high-ranked knight left—

—someone else came into the room.

He had believed without any doubt that a low-ranked knight would escort him out of the castle.

But the one who came was a man of far nobler station than some high-ranked knight.

It was an old minister wrapped in a dark cloak—Warren.

The air in the room completely changed. Warren had a clever and sharp air to him, making Anima tense.

Warren opened his mouth solemnly. "I know who you are."

He held a spear in hand. It was the magic spear that had been in Anima's house. The knight had worried he was still sheltering Brunhild and had found it when searching his house.

Warren spoke brusquely, but Anima did sense he was being clearly respectful.

"First, I must apologize. The old royal family should never have fallen on such hard times."

Having been a close aide to the queen, Warren also knew about the old royal family—and also that they had been persecuted to prevent them from attacking those who had supplanted them.

The Dragonslaying Queen had meant to safeguard the old royal family, before. Even after her death, so long as those vassals who continued to succeed her will had lived, the old royal family had been protected. But the aristocracy only cared about practical benefits, and they saw the preservation of the old royal family as no more than a waste of money. The queen had died and her vassals had died, and gradually, the protections for the old royal family had weakened. Warren had succeeded the queen's will and tried to continue safeguarding the old royal family, but after the queen's death, there had been many other matters to deal with in the kingdom, and ultimately, he had failed to protect them.

"I am partly responsible for the fact that you could never voice your name."

Anima was taken aback. He had never imagined he would have an ally he'd never even met.

"If you wish it, you will be warmly welcomed as an aristocrat. Someone of your stature shouldn't end his life as a low-ranked knight."

"…Really?!" Anima's expression brightened. Before today, he had always wished for a normal life. But if he could have more than a normal life, then nothing could be better.

"Truly. But I also have conditions. Though they are not very difficult conditions."

"What are they?"

Warren offered the magic spear to Anima. "I want you to take this spear and fight for the sake of the kingdom. Protect the kingdom with me."

"Huh…?"

Anima hesitated to pick up the magic spear. He felt like that had a different implication from becoming aristocracy. It seemed to him that if there was such a thing as fate, when he took this spear in hand, he would be swallowed up by that great current.

As Anima hesitated, Warren said, "Your true name is that of a hero. A hero will have a responsibility they must fulfill. In your case, it's to offer yourself to the kingdom. Become someone worthy of your true name."

"What should I do…specifically?"

"For starters, I want you to help me kill Brunhild."

Warren told Anima about the kingdom's secrets. Either he was certain Anima would be on his side, or he meant this as atonement toward the old royal family—Anima didn't know.

"That spear is magic. It's possible you could take the life of a child of God. I have high hopes for you. I even hope you will follow in my footsteps to become the guardian of this kingdom."

Warren thought highly of Anima.

Warren knew the truth behind the killing of the evil dragon one hundred years ago. Once, the First Queen had told only him.

He knew the dragon that had been called a foolish king had actually staked his life to protect the First Queen. He'd had the First Queen kill him after he had gone out of control as an evil dragon, setting her up to be not the wife of a foolish king but a dragonslaying hero. To Warren, the old royal family were people owed a divine debt. That was why he wanted Anima to become the guardian of the First Queen's kingdom, no matter what it took. That was precisely why he felt something fateful about this encounter.

But Anima was still undecided. "What will happen…if I refuse?"

"Are you in a position to refuse?" Warren's tone of voice took a turn, becoming severe.

He was telling him implicitly—that if he was to be a hero, then not fulfilling his responsibility would be a sin.

Warren leaned the spear up against the wall. "If you're prepared to wield this spear, then at that time, I would very much like to call you by your true name."

Warren left the room, leaving the spear behind.

Anima gazed at the spear.

He had no choice but to fight against Brunhild. All this time, he had gotten by giving in to those who were stronger than him. He should do the same here. This wasn't a situation where he could refuse anyway. Judging from Warren's answer when he'd asked "what will happen if I refuse," he functionally had no choice.

He knew that.

"I know that, but…"

He thought of the three days he had spent with Brunhild.

Her reluctantly eating her vegetables, her accompanying him for shopping despite her poor health, and her telling that poor lie at the end in an attempt to be considerate before leaving.

He thought it would be easier if it had been some stranger he didn't know anything about. Even though it had just been three days he had spent with her—maybe he couldn't call her a friend, but he couldn't think of her as a stranger anymore.

"I…"

Anima remained seated on the chair, unable to move. He thought that it would be easier to never come up with an answer at all.

Brunhild and the amber dragon headed for the old estate of the Siegfried family. The old estate was the house where they had lived at the time when the First Queen had been a priestess. After the First had become queen, her relatives had lived there.

They waited for the residents and servants to leave, and then Brunhild and the amber dragon attempted to sneak in.

The estate was heavily locked in order to prevent thieves, but Brunhild destroyed those locks with her power of Thunder.

They had come in order to search for documents about dragons. In the basement of the old estate were documents that had been written up by generations of Dragon Priestesses. They had deteriorated over time, so if you tried to carry them away, they would easily crumble apart. For that reason, they were unable to transfer them to the royal castle or the Academy, and they had continued to keep them at this house. Relations of the Siegfried clan lived in this house implicitly to protect these documents.

In the library, Brunhild found the documents she was after. They described dragon spells. In a gem necklace she had brought from another room, she made use of a chisel to carve in the charm.

The amber dragon asked her, <**Are you making another gem to return me to my original form?**>

The gem she had once given the amber dragon had been confiscated when he'd been imprisoned in the tower.

<I'll make one of those too, soon.>

The chisel came to a stop. She had finished carving the charm.

Brunhild hung the necklace around the dragon's neck. Suddenly, the dragon began to transform.

He turned into a high-rank knight of the royal castle. He was even wearing the same armor.

"Dragon spells essentially can turn you into whatever you like. I carved a charm that can transform you into a knight of the royal castle. Now, let's sneak in."

"I see. So then I take it I'll sneak in on my own, destroy Kriemhild's crown, and rescue her?"

"I can't let you go alone."

Brunhild headed to a servant's quarters. There were a few sets of maid uniforms—from the maids who worked here at the old estate.

"I will disguise myself as a maid to go with you. You would be in trouble if something happened and you were alone," she said, and she went into the servant's quarters by herself. After about five minutes, she came out. In a maid's outfit, Brunhild was quite lovely. She skillfully hid her white hair with a cap. If she closed her eyes, then she would look just like a maid.

Brunhild spun around to show off her clothing. The skirt fluttered beautifully. "So? I think it suits me."

"It suits you. You seem to be enjoying yourself, at any rate."

"I've always wanted to try on one of these. They're cute."

Even in an unfortunate situation, Brunhild never lost her cheer. Bernstein wanted to quickly save her from such circumstances.

The two of them left the old estate and headed for the royal castle.

At the castle, they were able to enter openly from the front. The gate guard bowed to Bernstein. His disguise as a high-ranked knight kept anyone from suspecting the two of them.

When they looked for Kriemhild's whereabouts, they learned she was, as expected, in the throne room.

The two of them pretended to be a knight and maid and went into the throne room.

In the throne room were the old retainers, the knights including the knight captain, and some maids and butlers cleaning.

Kriemhild, sitting on the throne, looked like she was in pain, pressing the crown. She was desperately struggling against the crown's commands.

"Kriemhild…!" Brunhild just about leaped out, ready to help her.

But Bernstein held her back. <Warren is here.>

The old soldier was in attendance at Kriemhild's side. Aside from him, there were also countless knights in the throne room.

Pretending to clean, Brunhild watched Warren for a while, but there was no sign that he would leave Kriemhild's side.

<It could be…that he's anticipated I would come to save Kriemhild,> she said. But she hadn't come to this place without any plan at all. <Wait at the nearby terrace. I'll be right there.>

Bernstein followed her instruction and headed for the terrace.

From the entrance area of the throne room, Brunhild called out to Kriemhild on the throne. <Kriemhild. Come this way.>

She had called out using the Dragon's Tongue. The only ones who could use this were the Siegfried family or dragons. The Dragon's

Tongue was not audible, so the soldiers of the castle couldn't hear it. It would ring directly in the heads of those it was directed to.

Brunhild's plan was to make use of the Dragon's Tongue to have Kriemhild approach her, upon which Brunhild would destroy the crown with her Thunder, meet up with Bernstein on the terrace, have him turn back into a dragon, and escape.

<Kriemhild.>

It seemed Kriemhild had heard her call, as she lifted her head. <Sister?>

<I've come to save you. Can't you somehow come to the exit of the throne room? If you do, then I'll destroy the crown and we can escape.>

Kriemhild looked toward the throne room exit. <I can't see you, though...>

<I'm wearing a maid outfit.>

Kriemhild looked around the area again and said, <Ahh, I've found you. I'll go over there right away. I'll make up some reason to get away from the throne...>

But that moment, Warren at her side said to the knights, "It seems Brunhild has come. Search for her."

<?!>

The knight captain and his subordinates began to search for Brunhild.

It couldn't be that they had heard the Dragon's Tongue?

Impossible. There's no way...

That was when Brunhild realized—Warren had been watching Kriemhild's face. He must have figured out Brunhild was nearby from the changes in her expression. So then he probably already knew they had conversed in the Dragon's Tongue. Warren had been aide to generations of queens. Even if he couldn't hear the Dragon's Tongue, it wouldn't be strange for him to know of its existence and properties.

Not only were the knights approaching Brunhild—Warren was coming, too.

This is bad, this is bad, this is bad...

Brunhild was panicking, but she feigned calm as best she could and made to leave the throne room. She was dressed as a maid. There were a few maids in the throne room aside from her. If she didn't act in a panic, she might be able to get through this.

So long as she stayed calm, she would be okay.

Or so she thought.

But she felt a powerful gaze.

Warren was looking at her. That realization sent shivers down her spine.

When the old soldier had said "It seems Brunhild has come," he had not failed to miss one maid acting just a bit strangely. Warren had already fixed his sights on Brunhild.

He was briskly striding toward her.

Brunhild's body cried out in fear.

Run—

Her body remembered the pain of being stabbed with his stiletto.

But she restrained that with her logic—or with emotion.

I can't come this far and then flee without doing anything.

Brunhild readied her Thunder. Warren glared at her right hand with hawklike eyes.

She fired the Thunder. There was a streak of light.

Her arrow, trained in hunting, would never miss its target.

Although that was only when her opponent was not an experienced veteran. The old soldier easily dodged the arrow of light.

"Just as I planned…!" popped out of Brunhild's mouth unconsciously.

She hadn't been targeting the old soldier with her Thunder.

The lightning slashed past him, toward Kriemhild—more precisely, to the crown that was on her head.

The arrow that never missed struck precisely through the crown, some distance away. There was a sound like glass shattering, and the crown broke apart.

Even the arrogant old soldier was shocked to see that. He turned around toward Kriemhild, watching as the crown broke into pieces.

Warren immediately turned back to Brunhild. And then, unusually for him, he muttered in a voice filled with hatred, "You vile…"

Brunhild had already left the throne room. She was running through the hallway, but there was no way she could escape. Because Brunhild was sickly, she was a very slow runner. She would be caught before she reached the terrace where Bernstein was waiting.

Men's footsteps were following from behind.

It's all or nothing…

Brunhild turned a corner to leap into a nearby room. She figured she would hide inside to wait for them to pass—by going into a closet or diving under a bed, for example. It was unlikely that would go well, but that was her only option now. In the first place, in order for this plan to work, the room she entered had to be empty.

There was no time for hesitation. She leaped into the room. She pulled such a mad dash, her cap slid off, exposing her long white hair.

And unfortunately, there was someone inside.

But was this actually good fortune? Brunhild recognized the man there.

"Anima…?"

Anima, sitting on a chair, saw Brunhild and stood.

"Brunhild?"

The two of them froze, gazing at one another.

"Anima, why are you here…?" She gasped. "It couldn't be that because you hid me…?"

He said with a bitter expression, "Well, basically…"

She considered before saying, "…If you want to escape, I'll help you." If something awful had happened to him because of her, then she had a responsibility to save him. "There is a high-ranked knight on the terrace ahead. He is my vassal, a dragon. You should ride him and get out of the castle."

Anima was no fool. He could easily guess that the dragon was Brunhild's means of escape. During the time they had spent together, Brunhild had said, "There's someone at the castle I have to go save." Her being disguised as a maid had to be related to that.

"But then you won't be able to get away."

"Never mind me. You saved me. I don't want my savior to meet an awful fate."

Anima felt quite pathetic. Right now, he was thinking, *I can meet Warren's expectations if I kill Brunhild now…*

He looked at the spear leaning against the wall.

If he picked it up, he could kill Brunhild.

Without realizing what he was thinking, Brunhild urged him. "What are you standing around for? Hurry…"

I'm amazed this girl can be concerned for another when she might be caught, Anima thought. And meanwhile, he was thinking to kill the person who was trying to save him, for his own self-protection.

Anima was beset by intense indecision. Should he kill Brunhild or not?

That was when the door opened, and a man stepped in—it was Warren. He already had a stiletto in hand. The knights followed next.

"Ngh…"

Brunhild moved Anima behind her back. Thunder was woven in the fingers of her right hand.

But Warren didn't even seem to be on guard. It was easy to dodge and to knock down arrows from someone who wasn't even a warrior. He could even neutralize Brunhild right this instant.

But he chose not to.

He looked back and forth between Brunhild and Anima and said, "This is a perfect opportunity."

Anima's heart thudded horribly.

Warren said to Anima, in a tone basically like an order, "Kill Brunhild. You will become a hero. Don't betray your true name."

Anima was frozen. He had yet to make the decision to kill Brunhild.

Brunhild's eyes were fixed on Anima—but not to beg for her life. She was looking at his face in attempt to figure out what was happening. "…I basically understand what's going on. Anima, take that spear. And kill me."

"But…you…"

"It's fine. I've already fulfilled my role. I destroyed Kriemhild's crown. She should be free now. My sister is no fool. Right now, she will be escaping from the castle. So I'm satisfied."

As Anima was still frozen with indecision, Brunhild told him sharply, "I don't know why you're hesitating… You're too emotionally invested for having been together for just three days. I hate lowborn scum like you. You and I are not friends."

"You…" slipped from his lips in an angry tone.

With that remark from Brunhild, Anima made his move.

He picked up the spear that had been leaning against the wall.

His body swayed as he raised the weapon.

Brunhild closed her eyes. A magic spear might be able to take her life, but there was no guarantee of it. She might wind up suffering and unable to die. She wished that she would find peace after a single stab, at least.

Anima muttered in a loathing voice, "…Don't give me that."

His spear flashed, thrusting forward in a magic strike.

There was a clanging noise, and a stiletto soared through the air.

The spear had repelled Warren's weapon.

Anima turned to Brunhild and howled, "Don't you give me that! Because of you, my whole life plan is messed up!"

He scooped her up with his free arm. Her body was small and very light. Then he continued to run off toward the exit.

Not friends, my ass. Anima gritted his teeth. "Men are idiots, you know… Three days together, and you'll have a friend."

Warren didn't just stand there and watch as the pair of them tried to escape. He pulled an extra stiletto from his coat and threw it at Brunhild.

"…!" Anima somehow knocked it down with his spear.

But of course, Warren would not miss that opportunity. He pulled out another stiletto, its naked blade already moving toward Anima.

The blade was already right in front of him.

I can't dodge it…

Regret passed through his mind.

In a few seconds, he would be stabbed by Warren's blade. He couldn't dodge the stiletto, and neither could he block it.

Damn it. Maybe I shouldn't have saved Brunhild without thinking about the consequences…

Anima could only prepare himself for the oncoming pain.

There was a hard, clanging sound.

He looked to see the stiletto lying on the floor.

That attack he'd thought he couldn't knock down had been knocked down.

"Huh…?" The most confused one here was most likely Anima, holding the spear.

The spear had moved on its own. It had struck aside the blade as if it had its own will. Maybe this was one of the reasons why the magic spear was called magic.

Anima recalled—his clan had believed this spear would protect them.

Warren immediately tried to stab him with a new stiletto, but the spear repelled that, too.

Its spearpoint danced—in order to protect the two royals from evil.

It was as if its former owner were trying to get revenge.

Warren swung a stiletto at Anima. In response, Anima manifested skill greater than what he had naturally, brushing it aside.

They clashed about ten times.

But neither of them could bring the fight to an end. If this had been an ordinary fight, the magic spear would have long since pierced the heart of its foe. But despite his age, Warren was capable enough to rival the magic spear.

The competition between the magic spear and the old soldier was intense, and the knights who rushed up to the scene were unable to interfere.

The sounds of weapons making contact rang out.

The magic spear gradually slowed.

No, it was the opposite. Warren's movements were becoming more precise. Warren understood the enemy's attacks, seeing through them well enough to lock blades with him. He had fearsome talent.

"You goddamn…"

Gradually, Anima was starting to be pushed back.

Sensing they were at a disadvantage, Brunhild pulled a little bottle out of the pocket of her clothes. It was filled with a silver solid and a fluid. She tossed it at Warren.

For an instant, Warren wasn't sure how to respond.

It should be easy to deal with. He could dodge it or cut it. But he recalled what had happened earlier. After he'd dodged her Thunder, the crown had been destroyed. Evading this bottle might be just what the enemy wanted—if she was throwing the bottle in order to get him to dodge.

Warren's conclusion was to cut the bottle down. He swung his stiletto at the bottle.

That moment, Brunhild covered Anima's eyes with both hands. And she also closed her own tightly. Anima yelled, "What are you…?!"

A powerful flash burst out from the broken bottle. The whole room turned white.

The bottle had been filled with chemicals that would create a burst of light via chemical reaction. The flash was overwhelming, blinding Warren. Only Brunhild, who had closed her eyes, and Anima, who had had his eyes covered, were all right.

Brunhild thought it would have been bad if Warren had dodged the bottle. If he had, then the bottle would have exploded behind him. She certainly would not have been able to blind him like that. Although she had thrown it anticipating he would choose striking rather than evasion based on their earlier exchange.

Now they could get away. Certain of that, the two of them finally made to leave the room.

But they couldn't.

The *shnk* of a sword's stab sounded in the ground.

A stiletto had been thrown to stick in the ground one step ahead of Anima.

"No way…"

Of course Brunhild would be shocked.

Warren had kept going—just as if he could see.

Even being blinded hadn't really hindered the old master's fighting prowess. He could generally pin down his enemy's position and movements based on sound, smell, and the airflow touching his skin.

Pulling out a new stiletto, the old soldier approached Anima.

His fierce attacks never let up. As their blades crossed, Anima was pushed back and back, farther into the room.

The entrance door grew farther away. Warren was almost starting to read the patterns of the magic spear's attacks.

Finally, Anima was cornered by the window.

He thought about leaping down to escape, but that was out of the question. This was the tenth floor. Below was stone paving, and they were sure to die.

But Brunhild cried, "Jump, Anima!"

"You've got to be kidding me…!"

Was she trying to say she would be okay if she fell, since she was physically invincible?

"I won't let you die. Trust me."

Anima had no other options. If he continued to fight Warren, then he would just be quickly defeated and die.

He had no choice but to trust Brunhild now.

"Damn it…" He smashed the window and leaped outside.

Warren did not follow. Of course not. If he did, he would fall and die.

Brunhild and Anima began to free-fall.

"Wahhhhh…!"

He had assumed Brunhild had some kind of plan when she'd said to jump, but it seemed that was not the case. Maybe she had tricked Anima in order to save herself.

Anima screamed.

But someone caught the two of them in midair as they fell.

It was the amber dragon.

"I called him in the Dragon's Tongue, telling him to come to the room."

As Anima and Warren had been fighting, Brunhild had been conversing in the Dragon's Tongue with the amber dragon. It hadn't been in human language, so only the two of them had heard it.

Brunhild smiled at Anima.

"So? Glad you trusted me, right?"

He had no reply.

Anima was passed out, foaming at the mouth.

Warren was looking down at the shards of broken window glass. They had completely outmaneuvered him.

All his plans had ended in failure.

The crown had been broken, and Brunhild and Anima had escaped.

He returned to the throne room. He thought that at least he would gather the fragments of the smashed crown.

He stepped into the room, expecting it to be completely empty by this point.

But there was someone there.

It was Kriemhild.

She was gathering the scattered fragments of the crown.

Reflexively, he asked, "Why didn't you flee?"

Kriemhild was a meek girl, but she still had God's Power and an invincible body. Without the punishment from the crown, if she was serious about it, she would have been able to walk all over some mere knights to escape.

"No matter what, I am still the queen. I swore to my sister—I wouldn't run from my responsibilities." While gazing at the silver fragments in her hand, Kriemhild replied in a peaceful tone, "And besides, I thought I said—that your inhumanity doesn't seem like it comes from ill will..."

Those weren't her only reasons. The events in the tower had also been a major factor. She figured if she hadn't seen him unable to strike her with his stiletto then, she would have fled.

Kriemhild offered the fragments of the crown she'd gathered to Warren. "Please accept this. Even if it's a cursed tool to me, it's a holy relic to you, isn't it?"

Those were the very words he had once said.

Kriemhild had assumed they meant this: It was a holy relic he could use to admonish the queen as he pleased, because it was convenient.

But now, it seemed as if that had meant something else.

When the crown had been destroyed, Warren had expressed emotion for the first time—feelings of hate.

No one would become that angry unless you destroyed something dear to them.

"Why is this crown so important to you?"

Warren didn't talk about his past. It wasn't worth talking about.

He pulled a leather bag from his coat, accepting the fragments and pouring them in as he said, "I just wanted to hear her voice—the voice that can be heard if you put on the crown."

They said that if you put on the crown, you could hear the voice of the First Queen.

But even if Warren put on the crown, he wouldn't hear anything.

The crown's purpose was ultimately to admonish members of the royal family. No one outside the family could hear that voice.

Warren thought—

He wished he could hear that voice one more time.

It would never happen—since he couldn't hear what he couldn't hear.

Though even if he couldn't hear it, Warren would simply fulfill its demand anyway.

Offer yourself to the kingdom.

Kriemhild told Warren, "I won't let you kill my sister. But I can't say for certain that your ideals are mistaken... Nevertheless, I cannot avoid deciding which path to take—because I'm the queen."

With all sincerity, she said, "Warren. Will you trust in me?"

"What do you mean by that?"

"I...think I will make an official announcement about the Miracle to the people. That will mean the return of illness in this kingdom. But isn't that unavoidable at this point? This ceremony is equivalent to human sacrifice, and I doubt it can go on forever—just as the evil dragon that demanded sacrifices was destroyed in the end."

Warren quietly listened.

"The First Queen is dead. We cannot keep the kingdom exactly as it was. I do not speak solely of the production of the Miracle. Foreign nations are becoming a real threat, and new forms of class discrimination are emerging. Isn't it part of the job of those who govern to speak honestly about what cannot be done?"

The reason Kriemhild had not fled, even after the crown had been broken, was in order to talk about this.

All this time, Warren had been protecting the kingdom the queen had made. He was supposed to be one of those who governed. Though his methods were inhuman, he devoted himself for the sake of the people of the kingdom. So she felt mutual understanding through compromise would be possible and making that attempt was the job of the queen.

"Please, believe in me...no, in us. I doubt we can build a kingdom as perfect as that under the reign of the First, but I promise you we will create a strong nation that can overcome disease."

After getting that far, Kriemhild shivered.

Warren was looking at her with icy eyes. It was a look of penetrating cold, enough to make Kriemhild recoil from her determined speech.

"What nonsense you speak."

She had thought of Warren as one who governed. That was her mistake.

"The First has passed away. That is precisely why those left behind have a responsibility—the duty to make the utopia the First created eternal."

Warren was a guardian of the kingdom, but he was no governor.

He *seemed* like a governing figure with concerns for the people, but he was something else entirely.

He grabbed her arm. The strength of his grip drew a short cry from her. "The crown may be broken, but I will still have you cooperate."

He pulled stilettos from his coat. Within an instant, their points had pierced Kriemhild's arms and legs.

"If I pin you with these blades, it will be easy enough to restrain you, even without relying on the crown's control. I will shackle you as well and toss you into the throne room. I'll tell the knights that your health is poor and you will be alone for a while. If I do that, then the right to order the knights will remain with me, the regent."

Kriemhild was afraid, but she looked Warren straight in the eye. "What a sad man."

A stiletto pierced her throat.

"That will prevent your needless chatter."

Warren left the throne room, locking it so no one could enter. He no longer sought any queenly ability in Kriemhild. Now that the crown was lost, he was only thinking of having her live a long life in confinement, in order to have her birth children—in other words, in order to make material for the Miracle.

There were two things he had to do.

One of them was to capture Brunhild. This was to kill her and make her into the Miracle.

The second was to capture Anima. This was to steal the spear that could kill Brunhild.

He had to give orders to all the knights and have them begin searching for Brunhild and Anima.

Warren also set out for the search himself. What he feared most right now was that Brunhild would have ridden the dragon that served her to flee out of the kingdom. He wanted to secure her person immediately.

Warren dragged Kriemhild deeper into the throne room.

"…"

From the shadows, Knight Captain Alois saw everything.

With the two of them on his back, the amber dragon alighted in a village a ways from the royal castle.

It was the remote countryside. Here, the knights should not be able to chase them down so quickly.

They got a room at an inn. Brunhild had said she wanted to have the unconscious Anima rest properly.

She laid Anima down on the bed. It was just the two of them in the room. Bernstein had gone out to get them some clothes.

After about an hour, Anima opened his eyes. "Why…am I alive? I jumped out the window…"

Brunhild explained to him what had happened after they'd jumped out.

"Ahh, that's right. Because I tried to save you, my life plan has been totally destroyed…"

"I really am sorry about that. You're free to complain to me as much as you like."

"Then I'll just go and say it…" Anima vented a variety of pent-up resentments at her.

But she listened, without giving him any nasty looks.

This seemed strange to him, and he asked her, "Why aren't you bothered by all this slander?"

"I mean, I was just really glad that you called me a friend…"

Anima blushed, at a loss for words.

"You sometimes have a nasty mouth, but at the bottom of your heart, you think of me as a friend. So I'm fine, no matter what you say to me."

He covered his face with a hand. "If you're going to be like that… then I'm speechless."

His silence then was charming to Brunhild.

After a while, he regained his calm and said, "Hey, after this… what should I do?" He wanted to return to a normal life—but he understood he was a fugitive now. "Now that I've pointed a spear at Warren…"

"That's not all. Warren is most likely searching for your spear. Since I destroyed Kriemhild's crown, it will be difficult to make her kill me. So the magic spear is the only tool that can get rid of me."

Hearing that, Anima held his head in his hands. The situation was even worse than he had thought. "Do I have no choice but to live on the run?"

"I won't make you do that. I will get you back your normal life."

"How?"

"Obviously—we should just defeat Warren."

They would either defeat him or strip him of his position as regent. Then Anima and Brunhild would no longer be fugitives. So long as that man held the real power in the kingdom, they would have no future.

"...It seems to me that the kingdom he seeks to build is no longer possible to actualize," said Brunhild. "I think we're already at the stage where we should think about a new path for the kingdom."

She thought the same as Kriemhild did.

Anima asked a very reasonable question. "Defeat him—how?"

After having been so talkative before, Brunhild now fell silent.

That made Anima laugh. "There's no way you can defeat a monster like him."

"I'd like to think of a plan. I want a little time..."

After that, they stayed in the rural village for a few days, but Brunhild just couldn't come up with a plan to defeat Warren.

As she was thinking, Anima decided to practice fighting.

He didn't really believe he could get any stronger in such a brief span of time. But he did want to do what he could. At the very least, he wanted to get strong enough that he wouldn't hold back the magic spear.

Bernstein found him as he was swinging around the spear until late at night.

The older man said to him, "You're sure working hard. But frantically swinging around that spear on your own isn't going to help you when it comes time to fight."

"Shut up," Anima answered as he continued to swing the spear. "I'll do everything I can. 'Cause that's all I can do."

Bernstein smiled weakly and said, "You're so young."

Anima didn't get the sense from that remark that he was being scoffed at. In fact, he sounded a little envious.

"I'll help you." Bernstein transformed into a dragon and stood before Anima.

That made Anima recoil. The amber dragon was small for a dragon, just over five meters tall, but he was still plenty daunting.

The amber dragon glared at Anima. Even Anima, who didn't understand the Dragon's Tongue, could tell what he was saying.

If you flinch just to see me, then defeating Warren is but a faraway dream.

That's what he was saying.

Anima swung his spear, and he began his mock battle with Bernstein.

Eventually, the time came.

Before Bernstein could think of a plan, the knights of the kingdom came to this remote village.

The knights were excellent at their jobs, and they'd pinned down the trio's location faster than Brunhild had anticipated.

Leading the total force of twenty knights was the knight captain, a man named Alois. He was past middle age, with a fine beard and an old gladius hanging from his waist.

The knights and captain came to the village at night.

Twelve knights swiftly surrounded the inn where they were staying—to keep them from escaping, no matter what.

The one to notice they were surrounded was Anima.

He quickly woke Brunhild and Bernstein and whispered in their ears, "We're surrounded. What's more, it's by some pretty strong knights."

Anima recognized the armor of the knights who surrounded the inn. It was armor worn by the elite dozen of the order.

Brunhild peeked out the window. There was a knight with a bow. "It seems they think we'll escape by flying away."

"We should do that," said Bernstein. "I'm strong enough to fly carrying the both of you."

"No, we won't escape via the air."

"Why?"

"If it were just you and I, then we could escape into the sky. You have your regenerative abilities as a dragon, and I cannot die. But if on the off chance they hit Anima, there would be no undoing that."

Anima got an uncomfortable look on his face. "Sorry…"

"Don't apologize. You've saved me many times… Besides, there's something that's bothering me a little."

"Hmm?"

Eyeing the face of the knight outside the window, Brunhild said, "I'd like to try facing them head-on."

"We've managed to circle them," a young knight outside the inn told the knight captain.

Ten of the twelve under the knight captain's command were stationed so as to keep Brunhild and her cohort from getting away. The remaining two would enter the inn from the front, along with the knight captain.

The knight captain nodded solemnly. "Well then, let's go."

"Yes, sir!"

Right as Knight Captain Alois was about to enter the inn, someone came out of it.

"Princess Brunhild…!"

Brunhild had come out the front door herself.

Her right hand was already wreathed in Thunder. It was pointed at Knight Captain Alois.

"Captain!" the knights cried.

Brunhild fired her Thunder. There was no time for Alois to strike back.

No—Alois chose not to strike back.

Instead of drawing his sword, Alois knelt before the princess.

The Thunder she'd fired had burned the ground at Alois's feet. Brunhild hadn't even been trying to hit him all along.

"…I tested you," Brunhild said to the kneeling Alois. "From the window, you seemed worried. It seemed to me that you were not very hostile considering you were here to capture us. So in order to make sure, I tried firing my Thunder…but now I'm certain. You all didn't come here to fight, did you?"

"You are very perceptive, Your Highness," Alois said, still kneeling before Brunhild. The knights behind him imitated their captain and knelt. "We have received the order from Lord Warren to capture you, but we have no intention of fulfilling that. We can no longer follow that man."

Alois was, despite everything, still the knight captain. He could tell at a glance that there had been no real hostility in the Thunder

Brunhild had thrown. But even if Brunhild had meant to fry him, he would still have fallen to his knees without attacking.

"The knight captain is the most honorable position in this country," said Brunhild. "Being in that position yourself, you would stage a rebellion against the kingdom?"

"...All this time, I have looked the other way and ignored Lord Warren's behavior. I knew that the generations of queens were being made into the Miracle and also that they did as they pleased with your royal mother's body. I stayed silent, believing it was for the kingdom's sake, but I fully recognize these actions were sinful. Everyone here is prepared to accept the punishments we deserve."

Brunhild's voice was cold. "It's rather late for turning over a new leaf."

"With all due respect, you are entirely right. But when I saw Her Majesty Queen Kriemhild's mercy..." The knight captain had been watching from the shadows as Kriemhild had gathered the shattered pieces of the crown and handed them to Warren. "Even after the punishing crown was destroyed, Queen Kriemhild chose to face Lord Warren. Even knowing his...no, our evil deeds, she was ready to forgive him."

"So she didn't run away..." Brunhild couldn't bring herself to blame Kriemhild. It was very like her, that kindness.

"Seeing her speak of the future to him," Alois continued, "I felt as if even my own heart were cleansed. I felt as if even my own sins were forgiven. But then that old man...he used his blades on Queen Kriemhild and locked her in the throne room. While I have been a disloyal man, I felt that I must save my queen if any honor remains within me...and so I hastened my way here."

"What do you seek from me?"

"Your assistance. Lord Warren is a fearsomely strong man. But the twelve I command are all famed knights. They are the best of those I have trained. If we all attack him, then we should be able to slow him down, at least. Please use that chance to save Queen Kriemhild and flee out of the kingdom."

Brunhild's eyes could tell if someone was lying. So she knew this knight captain spoke the truth. It seemed he was not trying to take her by surprise to capture her.

But Brunhild still had complicated feelings. "Frankly speaking, I cannot bring myself to have any affection for you all—since you pretended not to see as my sister suffered."

"I have no answer for that."

"If you feel regret, then now, in this moment, your lives are mine. Obey my orders. We will save my sister. But we will not flee. We will defeat Warren and take back my sister and the kingdom."

"Let me say most humbly," Alois said without lifting his head, "that man Warren is possessed of immeasurable strength. All the knights here are elite fighters personally trained by myself, but even all of us together would most likely be unable to defeat him. And not only is he a man of military prowess, but according to rumors, he has some means to make even dragons obey him…"

"Then I will lend my hand, as the Dragonslaying Princess."

"Your Highness standing on the battlefield would be very dangerous…"

"I will brook no arguments. Your lives already belong to me."

Alois seemed choked for a moment, but he immediately replied, "I will do as you say."

"Tomorrow evening, we will launch a night attack on Warren. I have high hopes for your work."

"Yes, Your Highness!"

As the knights were about to leave, Brunhild said hesitantly, "…I will offer my tentative gratitude. Thank you for standing up for my sister's sake."

"Your kindness is wasted on me."

That evening, the knights stayed in the village as well.

They were to return to the royal capital along with Brunhild and her friends when the sun rose and the horses could run.

When Brunhild returned to their room, she meant to tell Bernstein and Anima about her exchange with the knights.

But unfortunately, Bernstein was out of the room, so she told Anima first, "Bernstein and I will team up with the knights to beat Warren. You wait in town for our report."

Anima seemed a little angry. "Why am I the only one on standby?"

"I don't want to cause any more trouble for you. The knights are all very skilled. If I'm with them, surely we'll be able to beat Warren."

"I'm going with you. It makes me look bad when a woman like you is taking all these risks."

"It has nothing to do with being a man or a woman. Just wait—there's no need for you to throw yourself into danger."

"Shut up... I told you. I'm coming with you."

"I don't want to drag you into this."

"Agh, come on..." Anima combed through his hair fiercely in irritation. "Don't you quibble about whether you're dragging me in or not at this point. I was dragged in quite a while ago, and I've come too far to turn back. I can't go back and be a stranger to this now..."

"But I'm worried about you..."

"I'm worried about you, too."

They gazed into each other's eyes. Surprised by that unexpected remark, Brunhild was at a loss for words. She looked at Anima with eyes round like a cat's. He felt his heart pounding.

The silence that fell then was very much the awkward type.

"Well, that's how it is...," Anima said as he scratched his slightly reddened cheek. "Though I'm worrying more than I have to. I know full well that those knights are crazy strong. The twelve knights directly under the captain's command are famous. Even Warren wouldn't stand a chance."

"Mmm, they looked quite capable to me as well."

"That's right. So I shouldn't have to worry too much about you... but it's just in case."

"All right. Then I'll accept your offer. Please be my escort, just in case."

"Guess I gotta..."

Brunhild looked Anima right in the eye and said, "Thank you."

"Shaddap. You can't just out and say embarrassing stuff like that. How old are you?"

"I felt I couldn't disregard your feelings."

"...This subject is over now." He sensed the more he talked about this, the more at a disadvantage he would be. "All right. Then there isn't much time until morning, but get some rest."

As Brunhild was about to leave the room, Anima called out to her, "Wait."

"Hmm?" She turned around.

"There's something I just have to make clear." After a pause, he said, "What do you think about what Warren is trying to protect?"

Brunhild lowered her gaze, falling into thought. "You mean... about the Miracle, of course?"

"Yeah."

In order for Brunhild and Kriemhild to be saved, and by extension to free the Siegfried family from their pitiful fate—

—they had to defeat the man called Warren.

But that also meant the kingdom losing the Miracle of Life.

"I think Warren is trying to protect the kingdom as it was—the time when it was at its strongest," Anima said. "Though the way he's going about it is wrong, ultimately, that would save many people."

Anima knew the suffering of illness.

That was precisely why he was hesitant about making the Miracle vanish from this kingdom.

"Tell me—what just cause do you have for defeating Warren?" Anima continued. "Convince me..."

Brunhild folded her arms and considered before answering. "There is no just cause." She went on, "I don't want to die. This comes first, no matter what. I don't want to be made into the Miracle. I care deeply about Kriemhild, and I want to save mine and her children from that cruel fate... And plus, I don't approve of his thinking in the first place."

"Trying to maintain the kingdom as it was?"

"Mm-hmm. Since change is unavoidable." She stated her conclusion without hesitation. "There's no such thing as eternity. In this very moment, everything is changing—the kingdom, me, you, and Warren, too. This is what I think—you shouldn't be scared of change, but accept it. What's important is what you do then."

No matter how Warren tried, the kingdom was losing its old ways, bit by bit. That was an unshakable fact.

"If something permanent is impossible, then I'd like to move onward." Brunhild smiled wryly and looked at Anima. "What do you think? I do mean that to be my utterly sincere answer."

"It's no good at all. It sounds like you really don't have just cause."

"Oh, dear…"

Anima sighed and then said, "Maybe I'll be the town doctor."

"Hmm?"

"After the Miracle is gone. There are basically no doctors in this country anymore. So then you'll need one, right?"

"So I've won you over?"

"I guess… Frankly, so long as you were encouraging me onward, I didn't care about your answer. I have no choice anyway."

They had to defeat Warren, or Anima would have no future, either.

"How cruel! When I did my best to give you a serious answer." Brunhild smiled wryly. "If you're going to be the town doctor, then I suppose I'll be the jeweler." Her eyes were sparkling. "There's something I want to do. I want to turn the dragons in this kingdom all back into humans."

She was thinking of the amber dragon. Just as he had been, there were dragons in this kingdom locked away in dungeons or towers. The gemstones Brunhild carved could turn them back into humans.

"It seems like they'd struggle even after getting turned back," said Anima. "Humans who were dragons would probably be persecuted."

"I'll do away with that prejudice, too. Dragons shouldn't be considered scary creatures." As Brunhild talked about her dreams, she became more and more enthused. "I'll start by inviting dragons from outside the kingdom to engage in cultural exchange. Listen, and don't be too shocked—I'll bring a number of the dragons that are said to live in Eden. They're very noble. People will most certainly change their minds about dragons. In the future, I'll make this kingdom into a utopia of both people and dragons."

Anima had been restraining a smile as he listened, but he finally couldn't take it anymore and burst into laughter.

"Eden? A utopia of dragons and humans? You're dreaming."

"You won't know until you try."

Anima laughed in amusement and said, "True enough. The future you describe sounds nice. It makes me laugh."

"Don't laugh, I'm serious. A few hundred years from now, this kingdom will be a place where people and dragons can live and laugh together."

On the other side of the door, a man stood listening to their conversation.

It was Bernstein. He'd gone to speak with the knights to make an effort to understand the situation. Then as he had been about to return to the room, he had overheard the two of them speaking impassionedly, so he'd eavesdropped without thinking.

The two of them were still talking about their dreams for the kingdom. Hearing them from behind, Bernstein thought this was very nice. Having young people like this would make the future of this kingdom bright.

Whether the dreams they spoke of would come true or not wasn't really the issue. Their energy would invigorate the kingdom.

"Just…" Smiling, Bernstein murmured at a volume only he could hear, "Anima, I laid my claim on her first."

Seeing the two of them speak in such an intimate manner made the tiny flames of jealousy burn in his heart. He had lived a long time since becoming a dragon, but even so, it seemed he couldn't escape his human nature.

Bernstein looked up at the night sky from the window. A moon that was the same color as his eyes was sparkling beautifully.

Even the irritation of jealousy was mysteriously pleasant. Surely, those feelings were a reflection of just how foolish his beloved was.

The next day, the trio and the knights returned to the capital. Brunhild and her friends were under the protection of the knight captain, so they were no longer pursued by any knights.

They waited at an inn for the moon to rise. The plan was to launch an attack at night, right at midnight.

As they were waiting, Alois was clearing people out of the royal castle. Preparations were moving along smoothly. Now there would be no one there to get in the way of Warren's assassination.

They would be carrying out the assassination in ten minutes.

Alois headed for the great hall of the castle.

He would be meeting up with Brunhild and company here.

They would be coming in ten minutes, but he had told the twelve knights to gather in five. Even at the scene of an assassination, he couldn't be keeping the princess waiting.

The great hall was pitch-black. This was because he'd cleared everyone out—but still, it was rare for all lights to be out at the castle.

He'd have hoped to at least have moonlight, but the light of the moon which he'd expected to be pouring in from the windows was blocked by thick clouds.

I'll light a light.

If they gathered in the dark like this, they wouldn't be able to tell who was who.

Alois approached the light.

Tap, tap, tap.

The sound of his armor on the floor rang out loud in the darkened hall.

Suddenly—

He sensed a presence.

"Who is it?!"

He whipped around toward the presence.

A tall, shadowy figure stood there.

Because there was no moonlight, it looked like an all-black shadow.

But he could tell even from behind who it was.

"Lord Warren…"

The shadowy figure replied, "Alois."

Alois had served many years as the knight captain.

His skills were the real thing. That was why he instantly understood.

So our plan has been exposed.

If not for that, there was no way the target of their assassination would appear right before they were supposed to carry out the act.

He could think of many reasons the plan could have been exposed. One of Warren's men could have reported Alois for strange behavior, or Warren himself may have figured out that Alois had recently made a bold move in order to make contact with Brunhild. Or perhaps when he had seen Warren stab Kriemhild, Warren had also noticed him. At the time, Alois had worn an expression of clear hostility toward Warren.

The shadowy figure said to him. "Alois. You have been ardent in the education of the younger generation. You've trained twelve knights."

"Yes, when considering the future of the knights, one must nurture the next generation." He answered appropriately to the conversation Warren had started. He was hoping to drag it out as long as possible.

There was no way he would beat Warren on his own.

So he would wait for his allies.

Before long, his allies would be coming to this great hall.

Five minutes. If he waited just five minutes, then the twelve knights he had trained himself would come.

With them all under the same roof, they would be able to match this old soldier, with his monstrous strength.

Then if he could keep him another five minutes, Brunhild would come.

They had a chance at victory.

So he would buy as much time as he could.

The shadowy figure chatted on as if he hadn't realized Alois's intentions. "I never nurtured the next generation. I am no more than a genius...but no one could keep up with a mere genius. In the end, it was faster for me to do everything myself."

"Ha-ha." Alois laughed. "I envy that natural talent."

The shadowy figure looked a little irritated, and Alois tensed.

Had he said something wrong?

But the shadowy figure continued on. "If I had worried myself over the kingdom's future, then I would have regretted not having fostered the next generation every day for these past ten years. But happily, just the other day, I finally found him—a boy worthy of succeeding me. He is not only blessed by a weapon—though he doesn't realize it himself, he has martial talent. And most of all, his bloodline is fine. He was born to protect the kingdom."

"That's wonderful."

That was when the clouds moved outside the window.

Pallid light shone in from the cracks in the clouds.

That light made Alois relax a little. It was a mental reaction, due to the light shining into the dark hall. The presence of light in the darkness alone put him at ease.

The moonlight lit the shadowy figure.

"Do you understand what I'm trying to say?"

The color of the coat the shadowy figure wore could now be seen.

"If you're going to nurture the next generation, then you should make no compromises in quality."

Warren's coat was bright red.

Alois knew Warren's coat was supposed to be black, like the night.

So then this red coat meant—

Alois's throat turned bone-dry.

He hadn't even noticed that five minutes had passed.

Reinforcements would not come. Ever.

Because the shadowy figure had killed the twelve men.

He had found the most careless of the knights, tortured him, and then killed them one after another.

Alois drew his sword and cried, "Princess Brunhild! You mustn't come!"

It would be five more minutes until Brunhild's trio arrived.

Five minutes was more than enough time for the shadowy figure to kill Alois.

Fresh splattered blood soaked the splendor of the palace.

Right on time, Brunhild and Anima headed to the castle riding the amber dragon.

When they approached the castle, the amber dragon said doubtfully, <I can hear the sound of fighting in the great hall. Though it's faint.> He had better hearing than a human.

<It can't be they're already fighting...? Hurry. We'll assist them.> Brunhild pointed to the window of the great hall, and the amber dragon burst through it like an arrow.

Making a sound like a scream, the window shattered. The trio rolled into the great hall.

It looked as if it were covered in a carpet of red.

But it wasn't.

Red filth stuck to Brunhild's clothes as she rolled across it.

It was blood.

The hall was a sea of blood.

Alois was lying there.

"Alo...is..."

Brunhild was about to rush up to him but stopped.

Because she realized there was no head on his body.

Warren was standing there, illuminated by the moonlight.

In his left hand was a bloody stiletto.

In his right hand was Alois's severed head.

He was holding him by the hair, dangling there. Alois's face was in a foolishly relaxed expression.

Seeing the death of the knight captain, Brunhild understood all the knights had been wiped out.

Anima trembled.

"No way… The knight captain…"

Eyes like a hawk's looked down on Brunhild.

"This is what happens when you carelessly rely on allies."

With things like this, they had no choice but to fight.

Instead of a reply, Brunhild summoned her Thunder.

Or she was about to.

But Warren was faster.

Before she could prepare to fire the Thunder, he stepped forward.

In response, the amber dragon and Anima made their moves.

Warren threw Alois's head at Anima. The head of an adult man was heavy. He meant to wind Anima by hitting him in the gut with the head and disabling him.

Anima had never imagined he would use a severed head as a weapon, and he failed to react.

So his spear made to respond instead, but it was too slow—since the sight of a severed head flying at him made Anima's body stiffen up.

But the spear nevertheless moved.

The spear sliced Alois's severed head in two. That was a mistake. It had actually meant to strike it away, but the stiffness had gotten in the way. One half of the split head, the right half, flew behind Anima, but the left half struck Anima in the stomach.

"Guh…"

Even split in two with half the weight, the head hit him hard. Anima doubled over.

Now the only shield to protect Brunhild was the amber dragon.

The amber dragon came up to Warren to defend her.

The old warrior commenced disposing of the dragon. It was convenient that the dragon had come up to defend his princess. Warren saw him as the greatest threat of the three of them. The dragon was large and strong. Even Warren, with his talent for dragonslaying, could not beat a dragon in a pure contest of strength. Warren wanted to disable him quickly in order to keep the situation from becoming a brute-force struggle.

Warren dodged the dragon's fangs, then made to pierce his heart with a stiletto. The amber dragon blocked the strike with a claw. The tip of the blade deftly got between the scales to pierce the claw. He drew three more stilettos and threw them. He pierced the dragon's limbs with them. The dragon was pinned with the blades, just as he had been in their fight before. Warren's strikes were continuous and flowing.

Warren was about to go deal with Brunhild, the last one left. Brunhild, appearing from behind the dragon as it collapsed, had already fired her Thunder. The arrow of light she'd woven while he'd been fighting with the dragon was right in front of his face. But it was easy enough to dodge it, even at that close range.

But just this one moment, he couldn't do it.

In his heart, Warren clicked his tongue.

Alois…it seems you weren't knight captain for nothing.

There was a deep stab wound in Warren's right leg.

Alois and Warren were worlds apart in skills. Normally, Alois would not even have been able to wound Warren. But that would have only been if Alois were attached to his own life.

Being prepared to take the other man down with him had made things different.

In his final moment, the knight captain had given up on his life. He had chosen to give the other man a wound, even a minor one if he could, in order to help Brunhild and her friends win. Warren had misread the knight's determination. That was why he had taken a wound on the leg.

That wound kept his body from moving as he wanted it to.

He couldn't dodge the Thunder.

A crackling sound rang out, and the great hall was lit up white.

The Thunder had struck Warren.

Brunhild cried out quietly, "I did it…!"

Now she had won.

Or so she would have.

The arrow of light hadn't reached Warren's body. It struck his left arm and then dispersed.

"It can't be…"

Warren had defended himself from the Thunder with his left arm, wrapped in his long-sleeved coat. That was impossible. A coat that could block God's Thunder…

There was no way for Brunhild and her friends to know, but what Warren was wearing was not just any coat. He had favored this coat since his days fighting as a dragonslayer, and it was made from the coat of a magic sheep called Heidrun, which lived in a foreign land. Its wool was so durable, it surpassed even fine armor. The wool of Heidrun had almost entirely reduced the force of the Thunder.

Taking advantage of Brunhild's carelessness, Warren made to counter-attack. He drew a stiletto with his unwounded right hand and threw it at Brunhild.

The sound of flesh being pierced rang out.

"Urgh…" The stiletto had pierced Brunhild's right shoulder.

That made Warren grind his teeth. *I was aiming at her head.*

If he had pierced Brunhild's head, with her invincible body, it would have knocked her out for a little while. Warren had excellent aim with his stilettos—there was just one reason he had missed. He had thrown with his nondominant hand, his right one.

Having blocked the arrow of light, Warren had not gone un-scathed. While he had blocked the arrow from reaching his body, his blocking left arm had been burned, coat and all, and was no longer of use. And Warren was left-handed.

He approached Brunhild, who had been stabbed in the arm. If he brought the fight into close range, even attacking with his nondom-inant right arm, he wouldn't miss. He was thinking that rather than throwing, he would pierce Brunhild directly.

Seeing Warren come close, Brunhild internally chuckled. *Yes. Just like that.*

Warren's blade would pierce her. But that was fine. While she did feel pain, her body was invincible. As he was attacking her, Anima's magic spear would stab right through Warren. Then they could win this battle.

She glanced over right as Anima recovered from the attack with the severed head and was rushing over toward her.

Brunhild closed her eyes to prepare for the pain of the stiletto. Even if her body was invincible, she never got used to pain.

But the pain that was supposed to hit her never came.

The violent sound of metal clashing made her open her eyes.

"What…?!"

How could this be?

Anima was blocking Warren's attack toward her with the magic spear.

Finding this unbearable, Brunhild yelled, "Idiot! You…"

Anima cried, "Shut up! I'm sorry…!"

He understood just as well as she did—if he had attacked Warren, they would have won. But seeing Brunhild stabbed with the stiletto in her right shoulder and clearly in pain, he had changed his mind. No—perhaps it would be more accurate to call it an emotional reaction rather than changing his mind. Seeing Warren's stiletto coming in a follow-up attack, his body had moved on its own. His desire to not hurt Brunhild overcame his logical thinking and made him act. This was the negative side of him thinking of Brunhild as a friend.

His magic spear repelled the stiletto. Warren backed up a few steps.

Warren glared at the two of them, and they glared right back.

The battle in the great hall came to a brief deadlock.

Anima was the one to take a step forward. Warren met his attack. Blade and spear clashed.

Warren had fought with this magic spear once before. At that time, with his uncommon instinct for combat, he had largely analyzed the magic spear's attack patterns. He basically understood what sorts of attacks were coming.

But despite that, Warren couldn't break through Anima. While Anima had accustomed himself a little bit to combat in his mock battles with the amber dragon, the biggest factor was the wounds to Warren's arm and leg. The pain of his cut right leg and burned left arm threw off his concentration. Frustratingly, he couldn't move his right arm as he wanted.

But Anima was also frustrated. Even with just one arm, Warren was blocking Anima's attacks. There was no sign at all that his spear would reach the man.

The pair of them struggled, at an impasse. The only one who could change the situation was Brunhild.

Brunhild wanted to shoot Warren with her Thunder. But with the two of them in such a close and intense exchange, she couldn't fire her arrow. She felt like she might hit Anima. But neither did she have the skills to engage in a close-combat fight.

"Ngh…"

As Brunhild continued to look for an opening, there came a voice from behind her.

<Brunhild. Pull out the blades pinning me,> the amber dragon called out to her.

With a start, Brunhild went toward him and started pulling out the blades. If the amber dragon could move around, then they could finish this.

She began drawing out the blades.

Behind her, she could hear the sound of clashing blades. Anima was buying time.

It happened when there was just one more blade to pull out.

Brunhild felt an intense impact in her head. She lost control of her body and collapsed. As her consciousness grew dim, she saw it—a blade was sticking out from her forehead like a horn. A thrown stiletto had pierced her head.

"How…?"

But Warren had been fighting with Anima, and he wasn't supposed to have been able to interrupt them.

She looked over to see that Warren had sacrificed his immobile left arm to block the magic spear. He had deliberately let the spear pierce his left arm to block it, and he'd used that opening to throw a stiletto at Brunhild.

Lying on the ground, Brunhild struggled to draw the blade out of her head. But she couldn't manage it. That was because it was impaling her brain.

"Bastard…!"

Anima was attacking furiously. But that was actually not a good thing.

Warren could easily read such monotonous attacks.

This was right as Warren had already gotten rather used to fighting with his right arm.

"You're still green." He easily evaded the magic spear.

As the two passed each other, a stiletto pierced Anima's body.

With that, Anima could move no more. He wasn't physically invincible like Brunhild, and neither was he tough like a dragon.

The stiletto pierced his stomach, and a burning pain stole his will to fight.

"That hurts...dammit..." Anima went to his knees on the floor. Blood spread around him.

Looking down at that, Warren said, "Watch from right there. After everything is over, I'll heal you with the Miracle."

Warren stole the magic spear away from him.

Hard-sounding footsteps approached Brunhild.

Spear in hand, Warren was walking toward her.

Sensing oncoming death, she struggled. She floundered, trying to get the blade out of her head. But she wouldn't make it in time. She needed a bit more time to get it all the way out.

But...

...there was someone there to protect her.

It was the amber dragon.

He drew out the final blade that had him pinned and stood before Warren.

Writhing on the floor, Brunhild let out, "No..."

The old soldier was a dragonslayer with a magic spear in hand. A mere dragon was a shield of straw.

Warren looked at the dragon and spat, "Some filthy dragon, playing at being a loyal retainer?"

<Indeed. I've decided that before this girl, I will pretend to be a noble dragon.>

A human wouldn't hear the Dragon's Tongue, but the dragon replied anyway.

So then he had most certainly said it in order to make himself look good in front of the woman in his heart.

Man and dragon both moved at the same time.

It was such an act of domination that it couldn't even be called combat.

The magic spear pierced the dragon's heart. The dragon didn't even try to defend himself.

In exchange, the dragon captured Warren in an embrace.

In his last moment, the amber dragon thought—

How ironic this was.

Many decades ago, his life had been saved by the First Queen. The one to save him when Warren as a boy had tried to kill him had been the First Queen. While he had felt intensely lonely, being confined in the Academy basement, he had never considered suicide because he'd wanted to treasure the life she had saved then.

But it looked like he was going to be killed by that very same dragonslayer, in the end.

The amber dragon tightened his arms around Warren.

Warren thought that he meant to crush him in his embrace.

But it seemed he couldn't manage it.

With his heart pierced, the dragon didn't have much strength. His life itself would run out in just a few more seconds.

Warren just had to wait for that time to come.

Suddenly—

Warren felt pain in his chest.

It was a small, silent, but sharp pain.

He looked down.

There was a blade thrust into his chest. That blade was coming from an impossible direction.

From beyond the dragon, he heard a sniffle.

<I'm sorry.>

That remark in the Dragon's Tongue was trembling.

But there was no longer anyone there who could hear those words.

Appearing from behind the dragon as he fell was Brunhild.

"That blade…," Warren said.

Brunhild had gotten the stiletto out of her head and had gone right through the dragon with the Healing Blade to pierce Warren. This blade had magic-repelling properties. It was even able to pierce through the coat, with the protection of its magic wool.

Before the amber dragon had attacked Warren, he had said to Brunhild, <Pierce right through me.>

It had been the final secret exchange between dragon and princess. That had been the only way to defeat Warren.

Brunhild didn't like it.

She hadn't wanted to do such a thing. The amber dragon would have been able to tell she felt that way, too.

But the amber dragon had refused to back down.

To the dragon, who had lived through the ancient times, it was unthinkable for a child to be killed by an elder.

So he would protect her. It was the responsibility of an adult to protect children.

And so the dragon had come forward to protect Brunhild and immobilize Warren.

Seeing that the dragon's heart was pierced, Brunhild had broken through her doubts. She absolutely could not waste his sacrifice. That was why she'd drawn the sword her sister had given her.

"…"

Warren backed up two, three steps.

Blood started oozing out from the little hole in his chest.

He pressed his chest with his hand, and his hand felt the warmth of blood. His palm turned bright red.

The single stab from this blade that was supposed to guard lives was fatal.

Perhaps her strike had been a cursed one. Warren felt as if the blade had been painted in many layers of resentment from the queens he had used.

There was no way for him to recover—

No matter if he was a dragonslaying genius or a hardened old soldier.

His body was only that of a human. With his heart pierced, he couldn't make a move.

Warren laughed at himself.

"I see. So this is as far as a genius goes."

His body would no longer move. He couldn't fight.

So he was forced to use his last resort.

He pulled a white dragon scale from his coat.

He tossed it into his mouth. Instantly, his body began to swell.

The powerful vitality of a dragon started healing his fatal wound.

Anima, curled up on the ground, gave a little cry.

The kingdom's guardian transformed into an evil dragon—one large enough to fill the whole great hall.

The evil dragon bared his fangs and attacked Brunhild.

Brunhild fixed her eyes straight on the evil dragon.

She would not flinch.

She raised her right hand toward the dragon. Between her fingers was lightning.

<Becoming a dragon is a poor move against me, don't you think?>

The Dragonslaying Princess unleashed her Thunder.

The dim hall became as bright as day.

The flash of her lightning burned the dragon.

The dragon fell, shaking the whole hall. This time, he did not move again.

Brunhild dripped the Miracle of Life she carried onto Anima's wounds. With just a few drops, his wounds healed. In about ten minutes, he had fully recovered.

Next, she also dripped the Miracle onto the amber dragon's wounds. But no matter how much she dribbled over him, the amber dragon never began to move. Even with the Miracle, transcending death was the one thing that could not be done.

Brunhild embraced the dragon's head, eyes lowered. She cried silent tears. "I was entirely reliant on you until the end."

She kissed the dragon. His mouth could no longer chatter frivolously. The taste of death spread inside her mouth, and Brunhild sorrowed.

But there was no time to be indulging in sentimentality. She left the dragon's body behind and headed to the throne room. When she destroyed the lock with her Thunder and went inside, there was Kriemhild, pinned with blades.

Brunhild approached and drew the blades from her sister's body. Now able to move, Kriemhild embraced her sister.

"Oh, Sister... How incredible that you could get here safe..."

Brunhild stroked her sister's hair and said, "I'm sorry it took me so long. It must have been hard."

After sharing the joy of reunion, Kriemhild asked, "What happened to Warren?"

The sisters returned to the great hall.

There was Warren, sitting with his back against the wall.

He had returned to his human form. The scale that he had swallowed had been specially made, and after a certain time passed after swallowing it, you could return to human form.

Wounded all over, Warren looked up at the sisters.

He could no longer move, but he was still breathing.

With Anima helping her, Brunhild tied Warren up firmly.

Looking down at Warren, Brunhild said with loathing, "I hate you. You tortured my sister and killed my dragon. Frankly, I'd like to kill you. But…I will not do that."

Warren asked her in a hoarse, barely audible voice—that was all he could get out now—"Why won't you kill me?"

"Because the queen stopped me," said Brunhild.

Kriemhild came before him. In her hands, she held a small bottle of the Miracle.

While pouring the contents of that little bottle on Warren's wounds, Kriemhild said, "The kingdom I aim to build is one without hatred. I would like to make this kingdom a place that takes heed of God's teachings and has no conflict or hatred, like the Kingdom of Eternity. So…I will forgive you."

Kriemhild healed all of Warren's wounds.

"Warren. Your help is needed for the sake of my ideal kingdom. Please swear to me—that now, you will serve me, your queen. Not the First, but me… Please offer yourself for the sake of the future of the kingdom. So long as you swear, I will believe in you and undo this rope."

Warren fixed his gaze on Kriemhild and spoke.

His wrinkled eyes were gazing at the distant past. "Princess Kriemhild. Your black eyes…and your black hair…look very much like those of the First. But you are *not* the First. You cannot build the Kingdom of Eternity."

With a cough, Warren spat blood. That confused them.

"Why? The Miracle should have healed your wounds…"

Warren had hidden poison in his back teeth. He had planned to kill himself with it.

Warren didn't want to live at Kriemhild's side.

If the kingdom that the First Queen had built would fall, then he would simply share that kingdom's fate.

Kriemhild hurriedly made him drink the Miracle, but it was too late. It would take a few minutes for the Miracle to take effect. The poison would kill him before that. Now there was only to wait for the faint consciousness that remained in his body to be extinguished.

He could only see blackness now. Death swiftly robbed him of his senses. All that was left was his hearing and sense of touch.

In the darkness of death, Warren's body sensed some kind of warmth.

Someone was embracing him.

He thought it had to be Kriemhild. An inexpressible affection could be felt from her touch.

A very long time ago, he had felt the same sensation.

It had been many decades ago now.

When he had been standing there in the village square, the First had found him and embraced him.

You must have been scared, she'd said.

He hadn't understood what that meant. He was someone who would never fear. Even standing up against a dragon, he had felt no fear. He had been certain he would never fear anything until his death.

So he had thought.

But without even realizing it, fear became the only thing that moved me.

The fear of losing the kingdom the queen made was the one thing that controlled me.

He could remember it like yesterday.

Looking down on the perfect kingdom from the castle.

And shedding tears at its beauty.

In the darkness, he heard a voice.
"It's all right. You need not fear."
That voice drew Warren into the distant past.
I see. So it was her voice that most resembled her.
He only realized it after losing his sight.

When he'd been able to see, his eyes had only ever focused on Kriemhild's appearance.

To comfort the dying soul, Kriemhild continued to hold the old soldier.

Being in darkness, Warren felt as if he were in the First Queen's embrace.

Just like when they had first met.

A single tear streaked from the wrinkled corner of his eye.

Seen off by that voice he'd wanted to hear one more time…

…the old soldier became a corpse.

As Kriemhild embraced the corpse, Brunhild asked her, "Why would you show mercy to that man? He was so inhuman…"

Kriemhild answered her,

"Though the manner of it was warped…he always protected this kingdom."

I wished to make that kingdom eternal.

I
wished
to take
that
view...

...and
stop the
flow of
time right
there.

Epilogue

A woman carrying a baby was racing through the capital of the kingdom.

She knocked on the door of a private house and cried, "Please share the Miracle with me. My baby is ill. It's to save her, please... Even a drop."

There was no answer from within. The woman immediately raced to the next house. She knocked on the door and cried, "The Miracle..."

This time, she did get a reply.

"We've got no Miracle to share with you!" a man yelled.

The woman carrying the baby went around to different houses, one after another.

"Please, please..."

But nobody would share the Miracle.

Eventually, her feet came to a stop.

"Ahh..." She crumpled on the street. The baby had died in her arms. The mother's wails echoed through the midday.

The people walking along the streets pitied the mother.

"The poor woman..."

"If she'd just had the Miracle..."

"It's because of that foolish Queen Kriemhild."

"What a useless ruler, not even able to create the Miracle..."

Five years had passed since Warren's death.

The Miracle, which had once been used widely in the kingdom, had now long since become rare.

A man and woman were gazing at the mother whose child had died.

"What an awful sight to see…"

It was Anima. Over the course of five years, he had grown into a tall man.

At Anima's side was Brunhild. Her characteristic sickly pallor hadn't changed since back then. But perhaps because she was now grown, her pale skin had an unchastely bewitching edge to it.

Brunhild said, "…I sometimes wonder if what we did might have been a mistake."

Anima listened in silence.

"If we had left things to Warren, then perhaps that baby would not have had to die. There would still have been lots of the Miracle in this kingdom. How many tragedies like that are there now?"

"It's not only this kingdom that's like that." Anima disagreed with Brunhild's timid speculation. "It's sad for someone to die of illness. But that's an ordinary event. This kingdom has just gone back to normal. I think this would have happened sooner or later, anyhow."

"So then can you say what we did wasn't a mistake?"

"No, it's for a different reason that I think what we did wasn't a mistake."

Anima looked at Brunhild and said, "If Warren had won, then neither of us would be alive."

Brunhild smiled wryly. "If you put it that way…then that's true."

But Brunhild quickly realized something strange. "In that fight, even if Warren had won, I don't think you would have died."

Warren had injured Anima, but Brunhild recalled him saying that once the battle was over, he would heal his wounds.

But Anima said, "No, if Warren had won, then Anima would have died. I think I would have gone back to my old name and succeeded his role as guardian of the kingdom. I'm not strong enough that I could resist a monster like Warren on my own."

After a brief silence, Brunhild asked, "Hey, Anima."

"What?"

"I can keep calling you Anima from now on, right?"

"I don't want to go back to my old name at this point. I'm not used to getting called Sigurd…" Cheeks slightly reddened, he continued,

"Besides, I like the name Anima. It means *nameless* in the old language. It's cool…"

Brunhild pointed at him and laughed. "I thought it was a strange name, though."

Now he really did go red, hanging his head.

After walking awhile together, Brunhild and Anima parted ways at a crossroads. After all, the two of them had just run into each other in town by chance today.

Before separating, Brunhild told Anima, "Just so you know, Kriemhild wants your strength. She has many enemies within the kingdom and without right now. She's said she'll pay you handsomely."

These past five years, Kriemhild had tried to offer Anima a cordial welcome at every opportunity. She felt the old royal family should never have fallen to begin with, and she wanted to make up for what had happened.

But Anima had rejected her every time. He still continued to.

"I will decline most respectfully. I realized five years ago. I don't have what it takes to be a hero, after all."

Five years ago, he had fought Warren with the magic spear.

Anima didn't want to experience the pain and fear of that moment ever again.

"It's enough for me to have a normal life… You know that I'm the town doctor now. I wanted to help people in trouble now that the Miracle is gone. I get to feel useful to people, and every day is fun."

"I'm sure that's true. Then I'll send Kriemhild the message that you've refused again."

Finally, Anima said to Brunhild softly, "I'm glad I could see you looking well today."

After watching Anima vanish back into the town, Brunhild headed for the castle.

More precisely, she was headed to a grave behind the royal castle.

It was a grave on top of a hill. There was a nice view, and you could see all of the capital from there.

It was five years ago today that they had killed Warren.

It was also five years ago today that the amber dragon had died.

The amber dragon's body was carefully buried in a grave behind the castle. No matter how busy Brunhild was with her work as the queen's aide and as a jeweler, she came to this grave frequently.

<Bernstein.>

Brunhild offered amber-colored flowers in front of the grave and spoke to it—in a voice humans wouldn't hear.

<It's only a bit, but lately...I think I've come to understand what you said once about people's foolishness.>

Brunhild was going around the kingdom returning the sealed dragons to human form.

She didn't receive much thanks for it. As Anima had anticipated, the discrimination toward those who had lived as dragons ran deep. Brunhild was making efforts to do away with it, but right now, things weren't going well.

There were many times when she felt like the harsh criticism would break her.

But even so, she would not stop freeing the dragons.

<Everywhere I go, there are people who offer me love.>

It was just a few, but there were those who thanked her—the dragons who could return to human form, and those people who were secretly close with the dragons.

Those people would tell her, "Thank you."

Times like that made her realize her own—if modest—affection for people.

<If I could talk with you again, maybe I could keep up with an adult like you now.>

Brunhild looked up at the clear blue of the sky.

It was right as a great bird flew overhead.

<I'd like to walk through the town with you again.>

Her Dragon's Tongue vanished in the wind, heard by no one.

As she was visiting the grave, someone came to talk to her.

"Sister."

She turned around to find Kriemhild was behind her.

Brunhild thought she must have been visiting Warren's grave. His body was buried in the same graveyard. Brunhild wouldn't visit his grave, but Kriemhild would.

Brunhild saw her sister and said, "I'm glad you're well. I thought you would be thinner."

Since Kriemhild had become queen, it had been a string of ordeals.

She had announced to the people of the kingdom that they could no longer make the Miracle. With this alone, Kriemhild could not avoid being accused of being a poor ruler. Kriemhild had not revealed the secret of the Miracle's manufacturing these past decades to the people, so she couldn't explain herself. She'd made the decision with greater concern for the hearts of the people than for justifying herself. They wouldn't want to know the truth—they had been drinking medicine made from corpses. And then there was also the fear that people would become unwilling to drink what Miracle was left.

The queen took all the blame onto herself.

But Kriemhild wore a peaceful expression that gave no sense she was suffering. "There have been struggles, but when I get to see you, it gives me energy."

"I'm worried about you, Kriemhild. Take care of yourself."

"I'm all right. I won't make the mistake of making myself ill. It's for the kingdom's future."

"Most of all," she said, stroking her swelling belly, "it's for my child…"

Kriemhild was pregnant.

Her husband was the king of a friendly nation. The marriage had been arranged as proof of their alliance, in order to resist invasion from foreign nations. While the queen had married in order to protect the people, the people had not understood her motives. They said all sorts of things about her—that she was a whore sold to a foreign nation, and that she had dirtied the Siegfried family line.

But even being so vilified, Kriemhild paid no mind.

Because that would protect the people's peace.

The fact was that thanks to the alliance Kriemhild had built, attacks from foreign nations had greatly decreased.

Brunhild's expression was a little dark as she said, "There was no need for you to go so far as to marry."

"There was. I'm the queen, after all."

"But even so, a political marriage…"

"Ahh, you've been going around curing dragons and turning them human, so you wouldn't know."

Kriemhild smiled happily. "It's a political marriage, but we love each other, too."

The king in question knew of Kriemhild's devotion and had offered his support.

Having met a partner who would properly love her was certainly a rare happiness for this queen of many ordeals.

Kriemhild had the face of a mother as she stroked her stomach, her baby sleeping inside, with loving hands.

With that, Brunhild belatedly realized—*Without me even realizing... you've grown beyond the need for my protection.*

Before her was not a sister she had to protect.

She was a worthy queen.

That made her glad, and a little sad.

Gazing at Kriemhild's stomach, Brunhild said, "Let's make this a kingdom where that child can live happily."

Brunhild felt that now it was her turn to protect children.

"Yes," Kriemhild said with a nod.

She looked down at the kingdom from the hill. Gazing at the changing kingdom, she said, "Even if I cannot make the Kingdom of Eternity..."

After that, Kriemhild would rule the kingdom despite being vilified as a foolish ruler.

She spent her whole life devoted to the kingdom's prosperity, but the people never understood her love.

There never came a second queen in that kingdom crowned with the name of Kriemhild.

The name came to mean an uncommonly foolish ruler and was thought to be unlucky.

The dishonor would persist until her dying day and ever after.

The policies Kriemhild had enacted would become the foundation that supported the kingdom now that it no longer received the blessings of the First Queen, and this was not even known by scholars of later generations. Through the contrivances of those who hated the queen, Kriemhild's accomplishments were attributed to other queens.

Kriemhild's love became a sorrowful glimmer that was lost in the annals of the kingdom's history.

A fleeting twinkle, known only to her.

Afterword

It seems I enjoy writing villains.

That doesn't mean I love people who do bad things.

I love people who know what they are doing is wrong and yet are forced into doing it. You feel their humanity. There's the nobility in the attempt to follow through with their unbending conviction and the foolishness in staining their hands with evil deeds for that sake. When I'm able to write characters with both of those, I feel it, like *"Oh, I was able to write a person,"* and I come to love that character.

Brunhild is that character in Volume 1, and in the second, it's Fafnir.

In the third, it's Warren.

I feel that he's a difficult character, compared with Volumes 1 and 2. He's the villain, and he's not a handsome man or beautiful woman. He's an old man, and he does a lot of cruel things. As expected, my editor wasn't all that fond of him (this is not a complaint).

I was unsure. I wondered if maybe I should make Warren's character a little milder, in order to make Brunhild and the others, who really are the main characters, stand out more. Since no matter how much I like Warren, if the readers can't enjoy the story, then it's just self-indulgence.

But in the end, I chose to write a story that placed Warren in a leading role.

I remembered I'd begun to put together this story in the first place in order to depict his nobility and foolishness. It seemed like taking out all that would make the whole story a lie.

It's true that perhaps there aren't many people who will like this character. Perhaps it would be best not to highlight him too much. I'm sure these worries are legitimate.

But I felt certain of something else, too.

There were sure to be readers for whom this character would really hit home.

I decided to bet on this feeling of certainty. This is an issue of the point of writing a story. A story is not written to have people read it. You write not only to have it read but also to leave something in the hearts of the readers. If not, then I don't think there's a point in writing stories.

If this story could leave something in your heart, I'm glad.

Of course, I will also be very glad if you like the characters aside from Warren. I don't mean to have cut corners writing any of them. If there's anything else of special note, it's that I also like the virtuous Kriemhild in contrast with the villain Warren. I like to write about bad people, which also means I like to write about good people.

Finally, the acknowledgments. To Ningen Rokudo and Laila, who read this draft when they were busy and gave me their thoughts, thank you very much.